Bertolt Brecht: Plays, Poetry and Prose

Edited by JOHN WILLETT and RALPH MANHEIM

The Collected Plays
Volume Six Part Three

Brecht's Plays, Poetry and Prose
annotated and edited in hardback and paperback
by John Willett and Ralph Manheim

Collected Plays

Vol. 1 (*hardback only*)	Baal; Drums in the Night; In the Jungle of Cities; The Life of Edward II of England; A Respectable Wedding; The Beggar; Driving Out a Devil; Lux in Tenebris; The Catch
Vol. 1i	Baal (*paperback only*)
Vol. 1ii	A Respectable Wedding and other one-act plays (*paperback only*)
Vol. 1iii	Drums in the Night (*paperback only*)
Vol. 1iv	In the Jungle of Cities (*paperback only*)
Vol. 2i	Man equals Man; The Elephant Calf
Vol. 2ii	The Threepenny Opera
Vol. 2iii	The Rise and Fall of the City of Mahagonny; The Seven Deadly Sins
*Vol. 3i	Saint Joan of the Stockyards
*Vol. 3ii	The Baden-Baden Cantata; The Flight over the Ocean; He Who Said Yes; He Who Said No; The Exception and the Rule
*Vol. 4i	The Mother; The Measures Taken; The Horatii and the Curiatii
*Vol. 4ii	Round Heads and Pointed Heads
Vol. 4iii	Fear and Misery of the Third Reich; Señora Carrar's Rifles
Vol. 5i	Life of Galileo
Vol. 5ii	Mother Courage and her Children
*Vol. 5iii	The Trial of Lucullus; Dansen; What's the Price of Iron?; Practice Scenes for Actors
Vol. 6i	The Good Person of Szechwan
Vol. 6ii	The Resistible Rise of Arturo Ui
Vol. 6iii	Mr Puntila and his Man Matti
Vol. 7	The Visions of Simone Machard; Schweyk in the Second World War; The Caucasian Chalk Circle; The Duchess of Malfi
Vol. 7i	The Visions of Simone Machard; Schweyk in the Second World War (*paperback only*)
*Vol. 8i	The Days of the Commune
*Vol. 8ii	Turandot; Report from Herrenburg
*Vol. 8iii	Downfall of the Egoist Johann Fatzer; The Life of Confucius; The Breadshop; The Salzburg Dance of Death
Poetry	Poems 1913–1956; *Songs and Poems from Plays; *Further Poems
Prose	†Brecht on Theatre; *Dialogues; †Diaries 1920–1922; *Letters; Short Stories 1921–1946; *Writings on Art, Politics and Theatre; *Journal 1938–1935
Also	Happy End (by Brecht, Weill and Lane)

The following are also available (in paperback) in unannotated editions:
The Caucasian Chalk Circle; The Days of the Commune; The Life of Galileo; The Measures Taken and other Lehrstücke; The Messingkauf Dialogues; The Mother; Saint Joan of the Stockyards

* in preparation   † *not available from Methuen Inc.*

Bertolt Brecht Collected Plays

Volume Six Part Three

Edited by
John Willett
and Ralph Manheim

Mr Puntila and his Man Matti
Translated by John Willett

Methuen · London

First published simultaneously in hardback and paperback in 1987 in Great
Britain by Methuen London ltd, 11 New Fetter Lane, London EC4P 4EE,
by arrangement with Suhrkamp Verlag, Frankfurt am Main and in the United
States of America by Methuen Inc, 29 West 35th Street, New York, NY 10001,
by arrangement with Random House Inc, New York

This translation is a revised version of one originally published in Methuen's
Modern Plays series in 1977. A different translation by Ralph Manheim entitled
Puntila and Matti, His Hired Man was published by Random House in their
Collected Plays Volume 6, Vintage Books, 1976.

Photoset in 10pt Garamond by ⚠ Tek-Art, Croydon, Surrey
Printed in Great Britain by Richard Clay Ltd, Bungay, Suffolk

ISBN 0 413 47280 9 (Hardback)
     0 413 42320 4 (Paperback)

Contents

Introduction   vii

MR PUNTILA AND HIS MAN MATTI   1
  A People's Play

  The Puntila Song   94
  Notes on the music   96
  Editorial note   96

NOTES AND VARIANTS   99
A Finnish Bacchus by Hella Wuolijoki   100
Texts by Brecht   110
  A note of 1940   110
  Notes on the Zurich Première   111
  Notes on the Berliner Ensemble Production   118
  Notes on the Puntila Film   124
Editorial Note   128
  Preliminary ideas   128
  Scene-by-scene account   134

Introduction

On 9 April 1940 Hitler's armies invaded Denmark and Norway. Within a month the Nazis were in control of both countries. The Brechts felt they must move quickly. From Sweden, where they were living temporarily on the island of Lidingö near Stockholm, they wrote to the Finnish playwright Hella Wuolijoki asking her to sent them an invitation which would help them to enter her country. There they hoped to catch a ship to America from the arctic port of Petsamo before the next winter set in. Wuolijoki knew her prime minister well enough to persuade him to admit the author of *The Threepenny Opera* – a play that he had enjoyed – and by the end of April the extended family had arrived and found a temporary home in the Tölö district of Helsinki. Here Brecht at first resumed his final revision of *The Good Person of Szechwan*, the project originally conceived several years earlier in Germany. Then Wuolijoki invited them to spend the summer in her country house at Marlebäck in Tavasthus province to the north of the capital, where she farmed a twelve-hundred-acre estate. And there, while France was being assimilated and the Battle of Britain fought, Brecht began that short but intense love affair with the Finnish countryside which started a new phase in his work.

Their hostess was then in her mid-fifties, an old supporter of the 1905 and Bolshevik revolutions who was at the same time not only the successful author of some thirty plays but also a leading business woman, founder of two timber firms during the 1920s boom and thereafter chairman of the Finnish petrol company Suomen Nafta until 1938. She had been born in Estonia, one of those three small Baltic states which the Russians re-annexed soon after the Brechts' arrival at Marlebäck, but completed her studies in Helsinki where she met her future husband. Sulo Wuolijoki was then a leader of the Social-Democratic Student Union along with Otto Kuusinen, later to become the leader of the Finnish Communist Party and its

representative on the Comintern in Moscow. With them she took part
in the revolutionary movement, and when after the October
Revolution the Communists lost Helsinki to the Whites the
Wuolijokis were arrested and their house searched. The marriage did
not last long after that: Sulo Wuolijoki, it appears, became an
alcoholic; he was a big landowner and vile when drunk. His wife in
turn lost much of her political idealism when the First World War
broke out, so she later told Lion Feuchtwanger, and bought the
Marlebäck estate independently with her wartime profits; she also
visited Berlin where she met Gorky, Walter Rathenau and Gerhart
Hauptmann, and was a close friend of Ivan Maisky, who was to
become the Soviet Ambassador to London during the Second World
War.

Having done her university research on Estonian folk poetry she
wrote her first play in that largely suppressed language in 1912, only
to have it banned by the Tsarist censorship. Later she wrote in Finnish
(though she is said also to have been fluent in Russian, Swedish,
French, German and English) and during the 1930s had particular
success with her cycle of five naturalistic plays about *Niiskavuoren
naiset*, the Women of Niskavuori, of which one was performed
successfully in the Hamburg State Theatre in 1938 – until the Nazis
learnt of her political record. These and other plays of Finnish country
life and women's role in it became the mainstay of the repertoire of
the Helsinki People's Theatre (Kansanteatteri) directed by Eino
Salmelainen. And by the time of her meeting with Brecht in 1940 she
had also written a still unperformed play called *Sahanpuruprinsessa* or
Sawdust Princess, which Suomi-Film was hoping to make into a film.
This was based on an earlier story of hers which told of an authentic
incident of rural life that took place on her fortieth birthday, in 1926.
Now reproduced on pp. 100–109, it was called 'A Finnish Bacchus'
and featured the large-scale farmer Johannes Punttila (*sic*).

Brecht arrived on her estate on 5 July 1940 and was captivated by
its calm beauty. Thus his first entry in his journal:

drove with HELLA WUOLIJOKI to marlebäk (kausala). she
is letting us have a villa surrounded by lovely birch trees. we
discuss the quietness out here. but it isn't quiet; it's just that the
noises are so much more natural, the wind in the trees, the rustle

of grass, the twittering and the sound of water. the white manor house with its two rows each of eight large windows is over 100 years old, built in empire style. the rooms would not disgrace a museum. alongside it lies a huge stone building for the cows (some 80 head) with openings for fodder overhead for the forage lorry to drive to, and handsome water conduits, all in iron and magnificent wood, the reddish pine of the north. the winter in this year of war was very severe. so the cherry orchard froze, and thanks to the lack of rain this spring the vegetables are poorly. there is a small wooden house in which 14 karelians are living, fishermen and their families who were evacuated [in the recent Russo-Finnish war]. they pay no rent and get 10 finnish marks a day. h.w. thinks they manage all right on that. but they can see no future, their fate is being decided by parliament.

we are very sleepy; due no doubt to the unfamiliar air. just the smell of the birches is intoxicating, as is the smell of wood. between the birches is a mass of wild strawberries, and the children are exhausted with picking them. helli is going to have difficulty cooking, i'm afraid, the stove needs to be kept in and the water supply is outdoors. but the people are very friendly and h.w. has an unending fund of stories.

Already this sets the scene for a certain return to nature in Brecht's writing, and three days later he is visibly infected with the mood of *Puntila* and the Finnish poems (e.g. *Poems 1913–1956* pp. 352–3):

it's not hard to see why people in these parts love their landscape. it is so very opulent and widely varied. the waters stocked with fish and the woods full of beautiful trees with their scent of berries and birches. the immense summers that irrupt overnight following endless winters. extreme heat following extreme cold, and as the winter day dwindles so does the summer night. then the air is so strong and good to the taste that it is almost enough to satisfy the appetite. and the music that fills that clear sky! nearly all the time there is a wind, and because it blows on many different plants, grasses, corn, bushes and forests the result is a gentle harmony that rises and falls, virtually imperceptible yet always there.

In this spirit Brecht read the Greek epigrams in a German translation which his son now gave him, making him decide to write with the same formal tightness about more modern objects, whether military or domestic. He also read a number of books in English: not just detective stories for once but serious literature, possibly borrowed from the manor house. The work with Margarete Steffin on *The Good Person of Szechwan* came to a standstill. Everything was combining to reintroduce the author of 'A Reader for Those who Live in Cities' to that mixture of humour, harshness and simple beauty that he had absorbed so productively in the Bavaria of his youth. These he could find again in the landscape and people of the Tavast country, thanks to his hostess's shrewd eye and vivid gift of narration.

*　　　*　　　*

Hella Wuolijoki was not merely a knowledgeable guide to the new surroundings in which Brecht found himself but a writer who had managed in her own plays and stories to set down something of their essence. Above all she was a raconteur whose language and style exactly suited his socio-aesthetic tastes. 'marvellous, the stories wuolijoki tells', he noted at the end of July:

> about the people on the estate, in the forests where she used to own big sawmills in the heroic period. she looks wise and lovely as she tells of the tricks of simple people and the stupidity of the upper crust, shaking with perpetual laughter and now and again looking at you through cunningly screwed-up eyes as she accompanies the various personages' remarks by epic, fluid movements of her lovely fat hands as though beating time to some music that nobody else can hear. (loose-wristed, she beats a horizontal figure of eight.)

Steffin and Brecht began to transcribe her remarks and to help with the translation of some of her writings, which she seems to have been very ready to go over with the former. Thus there is a German version by Steffin of *The Young Mistress of Niskavuori*, one of the cycle already mentioned, which begins with Loviisa the young mistress and Liisu the maid carrying a big water bucket into 'an imposing farm kitchen built of wooden beams' – while Brecht encouraged his hostess to make a version of the traditional Estonian War Song which he and Steffin revised for her that winter; some lines from it were later cited in the *Caucasian Chalk Circle*.

The plan for making a collection of her oral stories came to nothing, since (in Steffin's words) 'If one takes down HW's stories in shorthand and then sees them in black and white it is remarkable how they lose their sparkle. Much of their charm is due to the repetitions and the lively play of her features, also to the beautiful way in which her gestures accompany them'. But in addition to the Niskavuori play Wuolijoki now decided to make a German translation of her as yet unperformed *Sahanpuruprinsessa*, which she dictated to Steffin, it seems, during August. Here was the Puntila figure whom she had termed the 'Finnish Bacchus': in real life Roope Juntula, a cousin of her former husband's who had indeed once driven his Buick away recklessly in the middle of the night to get legal alcohol very much as in scene 3 of the present play; he had also, like Puntila, got engaged to three village women, though this was omitted from her written version of the story. A number of other incidents or passages of dialogue in Brecht's text coincide (so Jukka Ammondt has shown) more or less closely with various lesser plays and jottings of hers, notably Matti's harangue to the herring (pp. 72–73) which occurs in a short piece called *Tramps' Waltz*. There is no doubt that these and the Puntila character, along with her vivid way of expressing his remarks, are at the root of the play which we print.

It was in the second half of August that Wuolijoki first began discussing plans with Brecht. To start with she told him about her projected play about Snellman, one of the founders of Finnish nationalism, thereby leading Brecht to realise that however they might agree about people and politics her ideas of the modern stage were some decades behind his. However, the previous year the Finnish Dramatists' League, with ministerial backing, had announced a competition for a 'people's play' to be submitted by the end of the coming October. Wuolijoki now suggested to Brecht that perhaps they might collaborate on an entry, and got Steffin to show him the new German version of *The Sawdust Princess*. This was not exactly the 'draft play' subsequently mentioned by him in his prefatory note (p. 1), since it was by no means just a first sketch but the result of much preparatory work. None the less he saw it too as technically old-fashioned and wanted to rebuild it along his own lines.

> what i have to do is to bring out the underlying farce, dismantle the psychological discussions so as to make place for tales from

finnish popular life or statements of opinion, find a theatrical form for the master/man contradiction, and give the theme back its poetic and comic aspects. this theme shows how in spite of all her cleverness, her experience, her vitality and her gifts as a writer h.w. is hampered by her conventional dramatic technique.

It was not just a matter of making use of her play's local colour and characters. He must dismantle its structure so as to avoid banal conventions (like the absurd happy ending), reveal the other side of the central Puntila figure, and infiltrate some of those spontaneous anecdotes which she herself would think hopelessly undramatic.

Brecht started revising and rewriting her script on 2 September, and within three weeks had typed out what he called 'a fat little calf of a play. it contains more landscape than any other of my plays except perhaps BAAL.' What he had done to change it, the stages through which he worked and the amendments which he made later, are all outlined in our editorial notes (pp. 128–155), whose main gist is that he made it into a rambling epic play rather than a 'well-made' one on Aristotelian principles, virtually eliminating the major character of 'Aunt Hanna' (though she still haunts scene 2 rather awkwardly in the form of the absent Mrs Klinkmann), and strengthening the element of class self-interest in Puntila so as to offset his drunken benevolence. He also brought in the stories told by the four village women as a result of the landowner's hostile behaviour (scene 8 arising out of scene 7) and gave Wuolijoki's cosy plot a downbeat ending by resigning Matti to the impossibility of natural human relations across such socio-economic barriers, except when saturated with alcohol. Alcoholism then, from being a national Finnish problem (which is how Wuolijoki seems to have encountered it in her own life), becomes an aspect of the class war, if still a broadly farcical one.

Not surprisingly, the initial impact on Wuolijoki of Brecht's alterations was a shock, for he had in effect taken over her play and in many cases her actual words, and turned them into something recognisably of his own: epic, Schweikian, schematically Marxist and in her view un-Finnish. But he managed to argue her out of such strictures, persuading her to translate the play back into Finnish and submit it for the competition, where it won no kind of prize. Thereafter they came to an agreement in effect to go their own separate ways. That is to say that Wuolijoki could dispose of the Finnish version throughout Scandinavia, making whatever changes she wished; thus she renamed the principal figure 'Johannes Iso-Heikkilä' to make him less identifiable with the still living (but now anti-alcoholic) Mr Juntula, and subtitled the play 'A comic tale of Tavastland drunkenness in nine scenes'. Brecht for his part could negotiate performances of his distinctly less jovial version anywhere else in the world, apparently without naming Wuolijoki as co-author, though he agreed that they should split the royalties equally. Yet he always regarded the play's Finnish setting, its relation to the Tavast landscape and its living legends, and its permeation (à la *Schweik*) with digressive anecdotes as essential to it. And if it owes its lovely background, its main characters and much of its humour to the warm personality of Brecht's hostess it also owes something to those anonymous figures whose photographs appear at the end of his and Steffin's typescripts: the Finnish farmworkers with their flat fields and wooden cottages, the women in headscarves at work in the meadows and the woods.

*   *   *

By the end of that September Hella Wuolijoki had made up her mind to sell the estate, which wartime transport difficulties were making increasingly difficult to run. Brecht had already turned to other projects – a play derived from Yamamoto Yuzo's *Chink Okichi*, to be called *Die Judith von Shimoda*, and a set of *Dialogues Between Exiles* based partly on Diderot's somewhat Sterne-like *Jacques le Fataliste* and featuring a working-class sceptic very like Puntila's Matti, whom he called Kalle, the name of a Puntila chauffeur in the original story and the early versions of the play. By 7 October the family were back in Helsinki, where they moved into three rooms near the harbour to await their American visas. These finally came through, along with a tourist visa for the tubercular Margarete Steffin, at the beginning of May 1942 ; she was described as Hella Wuolijoki's secretary. Brecht by then had completed the troublesome *Good Person of Szechwan*, written a new play in the form of *The Resistible Rise of Arturo Ui* and heard of the première, in distant Zurich, of *Mother Courage*, a work which he had vainly hoped might be staged in Stockholm or in Helsinki. At a late stage he had yet again to ask for Wuolijoki's help, this time in finding out about the cargo ships that might be able to take them to America from a Soviet port, whether Murmansk on the Arctic, Odessa on the Black Sea or Vladivostock in the Far East. On 14 May she and other Finnish friends gave the Brechts a farewell dinner in a Helsinki restaurant. The following day they left for Leningrad.

This was barely a month before the German invasion of the USSR, and once again the Brechts got away only just in time. For back in Finland the situation quickly changed as Hitler advanced through the Baltic republics and the Finns became his allies. In Karelia the Finnish army attacked, and by early September Leningrad was under siege. Wuolijoki, who had been involved in a last-minute attempt to keep her country out of the war, was now suspect as a Communist, a negotiator with the Russians, and a friend of Alexandra Kollontai, the old bolshevik Soviet ambassador to Sweden. She was arrested in 1942, when she was accused of giving help to a Soviet parachutist, the daughter of her childhood friend Santeri Nuorteva who, like Kuusinen, had been living in exile in the USSR ever since 1918. Kuusinen's daughter too, who had been working for the Soviet embassy in Helsinki, remained underground in Finland. Thanks to such associations Wuolijoki was tried for treason and imprisoned; she was all but sentenced to death – 'even though I worked far too little against the war', says an autobiographical sketch quoted by Manfred Peter Hein. Released after the ceasefire of 1944, she re-entered active politics, helping Herta Kuusinen to establish the Popular Front and herself becoming one of its deputies. She was head of the Finnish radio from 1945 to 1949, came to Berlin and saw Brecht's *Puntila* production with the Berliner Ensemble, and died on 2 February 1954 in her sixty-eighth year.

She must have been a woman exceptionally free of resentments, for she did nothing to assert her co-authorship of what is nowadays accounted as Brecht's play. Admittedly she continued to draw half the royalties – though Brecht may have intended this as a return for her friendship rather than an estimate of her involvement – but whereas she included his name as co-author of the Finnish version he never returned the compliment where the German text was concerned. The friendship itself seems to have remained unclouded, to judge from Brecht's letters and subsequent references to her, though he remained somewhat evasive in his answers to his critics on this point; thus it certainly is not enough to say, as he did to the Party paper in Berlin in 1952, that her play was 'in no sense the same play, but a different dramatisation of the same real-life events', since significant stretches of her dialogue were identifiably taken over by him. None the less it must have been a happy collaboration, and much of that happiness has become embedded in Brecht's text.

And yet he never seems to have made any attempt to get this play staged during his ensuing years in the United States, though as soon as he returned to Europe in 1947 it became one of his first priorities, initially in Zurich where he helped direct its world première at the Schauspielhaus (though for legal reasons he could not be named in the programme), then in East Berlin where he directed it in collaboration with Erich Engel as the opening production of the new Berliner Ensemble. The main adjustments made for the Zurich production were the introduction of the 'Plum Song' for Therese Giehse as Sly Grog Emma to sing in scene 3 (to the tune of 'When it's springtime in the Rockies' by Robert Sauer, 1927) and the virtual loss of the Hiring Fair scene; while from Brecht's notes on p. 114 it appears that he already saw the danger of allowing the audience to be so captivated by Puntila's drunken antics as to side with him against Matti. In the Berliner Ensemble production that followed, where the Puntila part was again played by the same actor, Leonard Steckel, Brecht took special measures to alienate him from the German audience, prescribing masks for him and all the other representatives of the bourgeoisie; later he re-cast the production with the smaller and more agile comedian Curt Bois in the title part, to reduce the old sozzler's human appeal still further. In addition the thinly schematic character of Red Surkkala was introduced as offering a 'positive', proletarian element to offset the much more interesting ambiguities of Matti. The linking 'Puntila Song' too was written for Berlin, where Paul Dessau for the first time wrote the music (after Brecht's death he was to develop this into an opera), while Caspar Neher came in instead of Teo Otto as the scene designer, contributing almost incidentally a series of splendidly lively watercolours of the play's main incidents as well as pen drawings intended apparently for projection between the scenes. This was the production that was seen by Wuolijoki and led her to tell Brecht in a letter:

> . . . and as for what you have made of Puntila, here we would never have known how to put him on the stage . . .

Indeed the Wuolijoki-Brecht version, though published soon after the end of the war, remained unperformed in any Scandinavian country until the year of Wuolijoki's death.

*   *   *

To Eino Salmelainen, who was well acquainted both with the history of its writing and with the previous character of Wuolijoki's work, the inherent conflict of style and of attitude at first made it seem impossible to produce. To modern critics familiar with Brecht's own contradictoriness this is, on the other hand, part of the essence of the play. For here he has managed to assimilate his own revived feeling for the unspoiled countryside, together with Wuolijoki's sense of anecdote and rustic expressiveness, into a thoughtful (and necessarily Marxist) analysis of the limitations of human geniality, of superficial warmth. To anyone familiar with the German theatre in Brecht's day it must recall *Der fröhliche Weinberg*, The Cheerful Vineyard, that notoriously jolly play with which Carl Zuckmayer in 1925 broke away from the prevalent Expressionism and at the same time distanced himself from the rebelliousness of his close colleague Brecht. There too a gifted dramatist had conjured up the beauties of the landscape, the vitality of an ageing farmer, the rejection by the farmer's daughter of an upper-class lover in favour of a man of the people, and even the humanising influence of drink; and had done so both decently (in the moral-political sense) and with great commercial success. Whether or not Brecht saw the analogy at the outset he must have realised that his had to be something of a 'counter-play' to this. And all the more so since Zuckmayer's great post-1945 hit *The Devil's General*, performed by the Zurich company eighteen months before the *Puntila* première, showed how easily the German theatre prefers any jovial, full-blooded autocrat to his unforthcoming opponent, whether in the person of Brecht's ironic driver or of Zuckmayer's inconspicuous saboteur. No wonder Brecht was so worried about what he came to see as Puntila's dangerous charm. Behind this Finnish Faust with his two souls, as also behind Zuckmayer's wine-grower and his Luftwaffe General, lurks the shadow of that spuriously genial, murderously popular figure Hermann Goering.

Contradiction, then, is the essence of this play, so that the great challenge for any director must be how to balance its conflicting elements against one another, thereby forcing the audience to discount the comedy and made a considered judgement. It is all the more difficult today since the Finland of the 1920s, which is where its original incidents were set, seems on the face of it so very remote from our world of sixty years later: remote from modern Finland, remoter still from Germany, whether East or West, and (of course) very remote indeed from Broadway and Shaftesbury Avenue. This was already one of the main objections raised in 1950 by the East German theatre critics, who forced Brecht into the kind of defence expressed by him on p. 123: the story, he claimed, was still relevant, even in a radically reformed society whose big landowners had been expropriated, because there too one could learn from 'the history of the struggle' and (rather more plausibly) 'because past eras leave a deposit in men's minds'. Yet are these characters and their conflicts really so very much in the past? Fritz Kortner, who was one of Brecht's closest actor friends both in Germany and in the United States, suggested in 1971 that it was ridiculous to treat the master-man relationship as if it belonged to a vanished feudal world: could we not envisage a contemporary Texan Puntila in a ten-gallon hat, alternately acting the drunken liberator to a black Matti or, as the sober employer, bawling him out?

Yes, perhaps we could, and one of Brecht's inspirations must surely have been *City Lights*, where Charlie Chaplin meets the drunken millionaire who becomes a different person as soon as he sobers up. Nor is depressive mania an uncommon malady in post-feudal society, though it can lead to extremes of behaviour quite as drastic as those fuelled by alcohol. But would Matti's Schweikian ironies be at all intelligible in the setting of *Dallas*? Hardly. Yet there is another society, in many ways much closer to our own experience, where just that type of laconic undercutting is a natural response to the wealthy grazier's social ambitions and alcoholically stimulated professions of mateship; where the outward appearance of democracy does little to cloak the realities of capitalist economics – what Matti's epilogue speech calls, in Lenin's classic terms, 'the old "who whom?"' – and where at the same time there is a wonderful, still underpopulated variety of natural landscape whose appeal is all the stronger since it is felt to be threatened. This is Australia; not so much the Australia of our own time perhaps as that of some thirty years ago, when the troubles of the depression years were still engraved on people's minds, and often enough on their lined and leathery faces too. Brecht's classic of country life in a harsh climate transports only too aptly to the other side of our globe, whose population is still linked, for better or worse, so closely with ours that we have come to accept its legends and its eccentrics, from Ned Kelly to Sir Leslie Paterson, as if they were an extension of our own.

Such a version is available, and certainly *Puntila* is a play that needs rescuing. For it is not a jolly romp with some amusing lines and characters. It is not a women's magazine story about the love of an only daughter for her father's chauffeur. It is not, whatever Brecht says in the prologue, a reconstruction of an extinct monster known to science as 'Estatium possessor', but deals with live issues. It is not a schematic conflict between ugly masked capitalists and open-faced workers. It is not a celebration of the Finnish national character, much though Wuolijoki would have liked it to be. It is something altogether subtler and more complicated than any of these things: a jumble of criss-crossing contradictions – Naturalism and epic theatre, the warmth and coldness of the two authors, the drunkenness and sobriety of their hero, the Finnish master and his strikingly un-Finnish employee, tranquillity in wartime, country beauties seen through a city-dweller's eye, farcical episodes making serious points – the dialectical list can, and perhaps should, be prolonged by anyone seriously concerned with its performance.

This is not to pretend that it is not also a very funny play. Unhappily in the present state of our world and our country's role in it, where we have an uneasy sense of fiddling before some great disaster comes, the British obsession with comedy has become neurotic. Today, as the media are continually letting us know, jokeyness is all; nothing like a good laugh, is there? – as if we were determined to go down the plughole not with a bang but a titter. Here however is a 'people's' comedy where the laughs are set against the dangers of the larger-than-lifesize personality, so as to remind us (among other things) of the other side of the folksy politician's television act. The play is unique in Brecht's work, and its balancing act between the farcical and the deeply serious is of a kind that ought to suit the British theatre better than it has so far done. Perhaps it is no coincidence that Brecht worked on it at a time when, for all his hostility to the British class system (and it is noticeable that he never seems to have applied for any permit to settle in England or the Commonwealth), he was reading a good deal of previously unfamiliar English literature – Boswell, Macaulay, Wordsworth, Arnold and Lytton Strachey all being discussed in his journal. This made him aware, apparently for the first time, of the great richness of the English literary and educational tradition as against the German, nor was it possible not to relate them in some measure to Britain's situation as the last country then holding out against Hitler. *Puntila* was actually written as the battle of Britain was being fought, with London in flames. Thanks to its unforced humour, at once dry and warm, it has emerged as the most 'English' in feeling of all his plays.

Not that this was for a moment what Brecht consciously intended. For as he also noted:

> puntila means hardly anything to me, the war everything; about puntila i can write virtually anything, about the war nothing. i don't just mean 'may', but truly 'can'.
>
> interesting how remote literature as a practical activity is from the centres where the decisive events take place.

It is a modest and wryly realistic view, free of all literary self-importance: the playwright just takes it for granted that he has to write, however useless this may seem to be. So Brecht went on relentlessly working, with the extraordinary productive obstinacy that was so typical of him, at the only true thing he felt he could do.

THE EDITORS

Mr Puntila and His Man Matti

A People's Play

*After stories and
a draft play
by Hella Wuolijoki*

Translator: JOHN WILLETT

Characters
PUNTILA, *landowner*
EVA PUNTILA, *his daughter*
MATTI, *his chauffeur*
THE WAITER
THE JUDGE
THE ATTACHÉ
THE VET
SLY-GROG EMMA
THE CHEMIST'S ASSISTANT
THE MILKMAID
THE TELEPHONIST
A FAT MAN
A LABOURER
THE RED-HEADED MAN
THE WEEDY MAN
RED SURKKALA
HIS FOUR CHILDREN
LAINA, *the cook*
FINA, *the parlourmaid*
THE LAYWER
THE PARSON
THE PARSON'S WIFE
WOODCUTTERS

Music by PAUL DESSAU

Red Surkkala's song at the end of Scene 9 was translated by
NAOMI REPLANSKY

*Proper names of three syllables are accented on the first syllable,
e.g. Púntila, Kúrgela, etc.*

Prologue

Ladies and gentleman, the times are tough.
Let's hope the future's made of better stuff.
But gloomy faces cannot set things right
So we present a comedy tonight
In which you'll find the elements of fun
Will not be doled out meanly, one by one
But thunderingly in hundredweights, like spuds
That tumble from the sack with earthy thuds.
Though we shan't hesitate to use the chopper
If characters get larger than is proper.
You'll see us re-creating on this stage
A monster from a prehistoric age –
Estatium possessor, owner of big estates –
A useless beast who idly ruminates
And still clings to dear life for all he's worth
A stubborn blot disfiguring our good earth.
Here you may watch him graze without restraint
Across the loveliest landscapes we can paint.
And if our settings leave you unimpressed
We think the words ought to supply the rest:
Convey the clank of churns beneath birch trees
A midnight sun above quiet inland seas
Red-tinted villages awake before cockcrow
Smoke rising up from shingle roofs below.
Such are the pleasures which we hope now are
Awaiting you in our play *Puntila*.

1

Puntila discovers a human being

Back room in the Park Hotel, Tavasthus. Landowner Puntila, Judge, Waiter. Judge slips drunkenly off his chair.

PUNTILA: Waiter, how long we been here?

WAITER: Two days, Mr Puntila.

PUNTILA, *reproachfully, to judge*: Mere couple of days, you hear what the man said? And there you are already packing up and acting tired. Just as I was looking forward to an aquavit and a bit of a chat about me and how lonely I get and what I think of our government. But you lot crumple at the least little effort, for the spirit is willing but the flesh is weak. Where's that doctor who was ready to take on all comers only yesterday? The stationmaster watched them cart him out; must have been around seven when he too went down after an heroic struggle, very incoherent he was; the chemist was still on his feet then, as I recollect; where is he now? And these claim to be the leading personalities round here; people are going to feel let down and turn their backs on them, and [*addressing the slumbering Judge*] what kind of a bad example to the locals is that, when a judge can't even stand up to a casual call at a wayside inn; didn't that ever occur to you? If one of my men was as slack ploughing as you are drinking, I'd sack him out of hand. 'I'll teach you to scamp your duties, you bugger', I'd say. Don't you realise, Fredrik, how much all of us expect of you: an educated man whom everyone looks to to set an example and have some stamina and show a sense of responsibility? Why can't you pull yourself together and sit up properly and talk to me, you weakling? *To the Waiter*: What day's today then?

WAITER: Saturday, Mr Puntila.

PUNTILA: You amaze me. In my book it says Friday.

WAITER: I'm sorry, but it's Saturday.

PUNTILA: That's not what you said just now. Fine waiter, I don't think. Trying to drive away the customers by acting surly to them. Now, waiter, I'm ordering another aquavit; listen carefully and don't muddle it up this time, one aquavit and one Friday. Got it?

WAITER: Right, Mr Puntila. *He hurries off.*

PUNTILA, *to Judge*: Wake up, weakling! You can't abandon me like this. Knuckling under to a few bottles of aquavit! Why, you've barely had a sniff of them. There you were, skulking under the thwarts as I rowed you across the aquavit, I hadn't the gumption to look over the gunwale even; ought to be ashamed of yourself. Now watch, I step out on to the calm surface [*he acts it*] sauntering over the aquavit, and do I go under? *He sees Matti, his chauffeur, who has been standing in the doorway for some moments.* Who are you?

MATTI: I'm your chauffeur, Mr Puntila.

PUNTILA, *suspiciously*: What did you say you were?

MATTI: I'm your driver.

PUNTILA: Anyone can say that. I don't know you.

MATTI: Maybe you never had a proper look at me; I only been with you five weeks.

PUNTILA: And where have you sprung from?

MATTI: Outside. Been waiting in the car two days.

PUNTILA: What car?

MATTI: Yours. The Studebaker.

PUNTILA: Sounds fishy to me. Can you prove it?

MATTI: And I've had just about enough of waiting for you out there, let me tell you. I'm fed up to the bloody teeth. You can't treat human beings like that.

PUNTILA: What d'you mean human beings? You a human being? Moment ago you said you were a driver. Caught you contradicting yourself, haven't I?

MATTI: You'll see I'm a human being all right, Mr Puntila.
'Cause I'm not going to be treated like one of your cattle and
left sitting in the road waiting till you are so good as to
graciously condescend to come out.

PUNTILA: Moment ago you said you *wouldn't* stand for it.

MATTI: Too right. Pay me up to date, 175 marks, and I'll call
for my reference back at Puntila's.

PUNTILA: I recognise that voice of yours. *He walks round
him, observing his points like an animal's.* Sounds almost
human, it does. Sit down, have an aquavit, we ought to get
to know each other.

WAITER, *entering with a bottle*: Your aquavit, Mr Puntila, and
today is Friday.

PUNTILA: Good. *Indicating Matti*: This is a friend of mine.

WAITER: Yes, your driver, Mr Puntila.

PUNTILA: So you're a driver, are you? I always say what
interesting people one meets on the road. Help yourself.

MATTI: I'd like to know what you're after. I'm not sure I care
to drink your grog.

PUNTILA: You're a suspicious fellow, I see. I get the point.
Never sit at table with people one doesn't know. And for
why? Because when you nod off they might rob you. I'm
Puntila the landowner from Lammi and a man of honour, I
got ninety cows. You're all right drinking with me, brother.

MATTI: Good. I'm Matti Altonen and pleased to meet you. *He
drinks to him.*

PUNTILA: I've got a kind heart and I'm not ashamed of it.
Once I picked up a stagbeetle in the road and put it in the
bushes so it wouldn't get run over, that's how far I'd go. I
let it clamber up a twig. You've a kind heart too, I can see.
I hate it when people keep talking about 'I, I' all the time.
Should have it flogged out of them with a horsewhip. There
are farmers round here'd snatch the food from their men's
mouths. I'd sooner give my hands nothing but a good roast.
After all they're human beings and want a decent bit of meat
just like me, so why not? Eh?

MATTI: Absolutely.

PUNTILA: Did I really leave you sitting out in the road? I don't think much of that, it's very bad of me, and I'll ask you next time I do it to take the jack handle and belt me one. Matti, you my friend?

MATTI: No.

PUNTILA: Thank you. I knew you were. Matti, look at me. What do you see?

MATTI: I'd say a fat slob, pissed as arseholes.

PUNTILA: That shows the deceptiveness of appearances. I'm not like that at all. Matti, I'm a sick man.

MATTI: Very sick.

PUNTILA: I'm glad to hear you say so. Not everybody realises. You'd never think it to look at me. *Tragically, with a sharp glance at Matti*: I get attacks.

MATTI: You don't say.

PUNTILA: It's no laughing matter, my friend. It comes over me every three months or so. I wake up, and all of a sudden I'm stone cold sober. How about that?

MATTI: And these fits of sobriety, do they attack you regularly?

PUNTILA: Absolutely. It's this way: all the rest of the time I'm perfectly normal, just as you see me now. In full possession of my faculties, master of my feelings. Then comes the attack. It starts with something going wrong with my eyesight. Instead of seeing two forks [*he raises a fork*] I only see one.

MATTI, *appalled*: Mean to say you're half blind?

PUNTILA: I only see one half of the entire world. Worse still, when I get these attacks of total senseless sobriety I sink to the level of the beasts. I have absolutely no inhibitions. Brother, you'd never believe the sort of things I get up to in that state. Not even if you're full of compassion and realise I'm a sick man. *With horror in his voice*: I become fully responsible for my actions. D'you realise what that means, brother, fully responsible for one's actions? A fully responsible person can be expected to do absolutely anything. He's no longer competent to look after his children's interests, he's lost all feelings of friendship; trample over his own dead body, he would. That's because he's fully responsible for his actions, as the law puts it.

MATTI: Can't you do anything to stop these attacks?

PUNTILA: I do all that's humanly possible, brother. *He grips his glass.* Here you are, my one medicine. I knock it back unflinching, and not just a baby's dose, believe you me. If there's one thing I can say for myself it's that I tackle these bouts of senseless sobriety like a man. But what's the use? Sobriety keeps getting the upper hand. Look at the lack of consideration I've shown you, such a splendid fellow. Here, have some of this beef. I'd like to know what good wind brought you my way. What made you come to me?

MATTI: Losing my last job by no fault of my own.

PUNTILA: How was that?

MATTI: I kept seeing ghosts.

PUNTILA: Real ones?

MATTI, *shrugging his shoulders*: They couldn't understand. There hadn't been any ghosts on Mr Pappmann's estate before I came. If you ask me I think it was the food. You see, when people have a lot of heavy dough lying on their stomachs they're apt to have heavy dreams, nightmares quite often. Bad cooking disagrees with me particularly. I thought about packing it in, but I hadn't any other job to go to and felt a bit depressed, so I made a few scary remarks in the kitchen and it wasn't long before the girls started seeing babies' heads on the fences at night and giving their notice. Or there was a grey ball which came rolling out of the cowshed like a head, so as soon as the stable girl heard my description she was took queer. And the parlourmaid left after I'd seen a dark man one night around eleven walking past the bath hut with his head tucked under his arm asking me for a light. Mr Pappmann started bawling me out, saying it was all my fault and I was scaring the staff into leaving and there were no ghosts on his place. But when I told him how I twice saw a ghost climbing out of the maid's window and into his own when the missis was in hospital having her baby there wasn't much he could say. Still, he sacked me all the same. Last thing before going I told him I thought if he could get the cooking improved the ghosts on the estate might lay off, 'cause they're supposed not to abide the smell of meat.

PUNTILA: So the only reason you lost your job was that they were scamping on the staff's food. I shan't hold it against you if you like eating well, so long as you drive my tractor properly and know your place and render unto Puntila the things that are Puntila's. There's plenty for all, nobody goes short of wood in a forest, do they? We can all get along together, everyone can get along with Puntila. *He sings*:

> 'Dear child, why sue me when you said
> We always felt so close in bed?'

Ah, how Puntila would love to be chopping down the birch trees with you, and digging the stones out of the fields and driving the tractor. But will they let him? Right at the start they stuck me in a stiff collar, and so far it's worn down two of my chins. It's not done for daddy to plough; it's not done for daddy to goose the maids; it's not done for daddy to have his coffee with the men. But now I'm doing away with 'not done', and I'm driving over to Kurgela to get my daughter hitched to the Attaché, and after that I'll take my meals in my shirtsleeves with nobody to watch over me, because old Klinckmann will shut up, I'll fuck her and that'll be an end of it. And I'll raise wages all round, for the world is a big place and I shan't give up my forest and there'll be enough for you all and enough for the master of Puntila Hall too.

MATTI, *after laughing long and loud*: Right you are, just you calm down and we'll wake his honour the judge. Careful though, or he'll get such a fright he'll sentence us to a hundred years.

PUNTILA: I want to be sure there's no gulf between us any longer. Tell me there's no gulf.

MATTI: I take that as an order, Mr Puntila: there's no gulf.

PUNTILA: We have to talk about money, brother.

MATTI: Absolutely.

PUNTILA: But talking about money is sordid.

MATTI: Then we won't talk about money.

PUNTILA: Wrong. For why shouldn't we talk about money, I ask you. Aren't we free individuals?

MATTI: No.

PUNTILA: There you are. And as free individuals we're free to do what we want, and what we want at the moment is to be sordid. Because what we got to do is drum up a dowry for my only child; and that's a problem to be looked at without flinching – cool, calm, and drunk. I see two choices: sell my forest or sell myself. Which would you say?

MATTI: I'd never dream of selling myself if I could sell a forest.

PUNTILA: What, sell that forest? You're a profound disappointment to me, brother. Don't you know what a forest is? Is a forest simply ten thousand cords of wood? Or is it a verdant delight for all mankind? And here you are, proposing to sell a verdant delight for all mankind. Shame on you.

MATTI: Then do the other thing.

PUNTILA: *Et tu, Brute?* Do you really want me to sell myself?

MATTI: What kind of selling have you in mind?

PUNTILA: Mrs Klinckmann.

MATTI: Out at Kurgela, where we're going? The Attaché's aunty?

PUNTILA: She fancies me.

MATTI: So you're thinking of selling your body to her? That's hair-raising.

PUNTILA: Not a bit. But what price freedom, brother? I think I'd better sacrifice myself all the same. After all, what do I amount to?

MATTI: Too right.

The Judge wakes up, gropes for a non-existent bell and rings it.

THE JUDGE: Silence in court!

PUNTILA: He's asleep, so he thinks he must be in court. Brother, you've just settled the problem which is the more valuable, a forest like my forest or a human being like myself. You're a wonderful fellow. Here, take my wallet and pay for the drinks, and put it in your pocket, I'd only lose it. *Indicating the Judge*: Pick him up, get him out of here. I'm always losing things. I wish I had nothing, that's what I'd like best. Money stinks, remember. That's my ideal, to have nothing, just you and me hiking across Finland on foot or maybe in a little two-seater, nobody would grudge us the drop of petrol we'd need, and every so often when we felt tired we'd turn into a pub like this one and have one for the road, that's something you could do blindfold, brother.

They leave, Matti carrying the Judge.

2

Eva

Entrance hall of the Kurgela manor house. Eva Puntila is waiting for her father and eating chocolates. Eino Silakka, the Attaché, appears at the head of the stairs. He is very sleepy.

EVA: No wonder Mrs Klinckmann got fed up waiting.

THE ATTACHÉ: My aunt is never fed up for long. I have telephoned again for news of them. A car passed through Kirchendorf with two rowdy men in it.

EVA: That'll be them. One good thing, I can always pick out my father anywhere. Whenever there's been someone chasing a farmhand with a pitchfork or giving a cottager's widow a Cadillac it's got to be father.

THE ATTACHÉ: *Enfin*, he's not at Puntila Hall. I just don't like scandal. I may not have much head for figures or how many gallons of milk we export to Lithuania – I don't drink the stuff myself – but I am exceedingly sensitive to any breath of scandal. When the First Secretary at the French embassy in London leant across the table after his eighth cognac and called the Duchess of Catrumple an old whore I instantly foresaw a scandal. And I was proved right. I think that's them arriving now. I'm a little tired, dear. Would you excuse me if I went up to my room? *Exit rapidly.*

Great commotion. Enter Puntila, Judge and Matti.

PUNTILA: Here we are. But don't you bother about us, no need to wake anyone, we'll just have a quiet bottle together and go to bed. Happy?

EVA: We expected you three days ago.

PUNTILA: Got held up, but we've brought everything with us. Matti, unload the bag. I hope you kept it on your knee the whole time so nothing got broken, or we'll thirst to death in this place. We knew you'd be waiting, so we didn't dawdle.

THE JUDGE: May I offer my congratulations, Eva?

EVA: Daddy, it's too bad of you. Here I am, been sitting around for a week now in a strange house with nothing but an old book and the Attaché and his aunt, and I'm bored to tears.

PUNTILA: We didn't dawdle. I kept pressing on, saying we mustn't sit on our bottoms, the Attaché and I still have one or two points to settle about the engagement, and I was glad you were with the Attaché so you had company while we got held up. Look out for that suitcase, Matti, we don't want accidents. *With infinite care he helps Matti to set down the case.*

THE JUDGE: I hope the way you grumble about being left alone with the Attaché doesn't mean you've been quarrelling with him.

EVA: Oh, I don't know. He's not the sort of person you can quarrel with.

THE JUDGE: Puntila, your daughter doesn't strike me as being all that enthusiastic. Here she is, saying the Attaché's not a man you can quarrel with. I tried a divorce case once where the wife complained that her husband never belted her when she threw the lamp at him. She felt neglected.

PUNTILA: There we are. Another successful operation. Anything Puntila puts his hand to is a success. Not happy, eh? If you ask me I'd say dump the Attaché. He's not a man.

EVA, *as Matti is standing there grinning*: I merely said I wasn't certain if the Attaché was all that amusing on his own.

PUNTILA: Just what I was saying. Take Matti. Any woman, find him amusing.

EVA: You're impossible, Daddy. All I said was that I wasn't certain. *To Matti*: Take that suitcase upstairs.

PUNTILA: Just a minute. Not till you've unpacked a bottle or two. You and me have got to get together over a bottle and discuss if the Attaché suits me. At least he'll have had time to propose to you by now.

EVA: No, he has not proposed, we didn't talk about that kind of thing. *To Matti*: That case stays shut.

PUNTILA: Good God, not proposed! After three days? What on earth were the pair of you up to? That doesn't say much for the fellow. I get engaged in three minutes flat. Wake him up and I'll fetch the cook and show him how to get engaged in two shakes of a lamb's tail. Fish out those bottles, the Burgundy; no, let's have the liqueur.

EVA: No, no more drinking for you. *To Matti*: Take it to my bedroom, second door on the right.

PUNTILA, *in alarm, as Matti picks up the case*: Really, Eva, that's not very nice of you. You can't deny your father his right to a thirst. I swear all I want to do is empty a bottle peacefully with the cook or the parlourmaid and Fredrik here too, he's still thirsty, have a heart.

EVA: That's why I stayed up: to stop you waking the domestic staff.

PUNTILA: I bet old Klinckmann would be happy to sit up with me a bit – come to think of it, where is she? – Freddie's tired anyway, he can go to bed and I'll talk things over with old Ma Klinckmann, that's something I meant to do anyway, we've always fancied each other.

EVA: I wish you'd try to pull yourself together. Mrs Klinckmann's angry enough already at your getting here three days late; I don't suppose you'll see her tomorrow at all.

PUNTILA: I'll give her a knock on her door and straighten matters out. I know how to handle her; you don't understand that sort of thing yet, Eva.

EVA: What I do understand is that no woman is going to want to sit with you in that condition. *To Matti*: You're to take that case upstairs. Those three days were the end.

PUNTILA: Eva, do be reasonable. If you don't want me to go up to her room, then get hold of that little buxom thing, housekeeper isn't she? and I'll have a talk with her.

EVA: Don't push things too far, Daddy, unless you want me to carry the case upstairs myself and accidentally drop it. *Puntila stands there appalled. Matti carries the suitcase off. Eva follows him.*

PUNTILA, *quietly*: So that's how children treat their fathers. *Shaken, he turns to walk off.* Come along, Freddie.

THE JUDGE: What are you up to, Jack?

PUNTILA: I'm clearing out, I don't like it here. Here am I, hurrying all I'm worth and arriving late at night, and what kind of a loving welcome do I get? Remember the Prodigal Son, Freddie, but what if there'd been no fatted calf, just cold reproaches? I'm clearing out.

THE JUDGE: Where to?

PUNTILA: It beats me how you can ask that. Didn't you see my own daughter deny me a drink? Forcing me out into the night to see who will let me have a bottle or two?

THE JUDGE: Be sensible, Puntila, you won't get alcohol anywhere at half past two in the morning. Serving or selling liquor without a licence is not legal.

PUNTILA: So you're deserting me too? So I can't get legal liquor? I'll show you how I can get legal liquor, day or night.

EVA, *reappearing at the top of the stairs*: Take that coat off at once, Daddy.

PUNTILA: Shut up, Eva, and honour thy father and thy mother that thy days may be long upon the land. A nice house this, I don't think, where they hang up the visitor's guts to dry like underwear. And not getting a woman! I'll show you if I get a woman or not! You tell old Klinckmann I can do without her. I say she's the foolish virgin who's got no oil in her lamp. And now I shall drive off so that the earth resoundeth and all the curves straighten out in terror. *Exit.*

EVA, *coming downstairs*: Stop your master, do you hear?

MATTI, *appearing behind her*: Too late. He's too nippy for me.

THE JUDGE: I don't think I shall wait up for him. I'm not as young as I was, Eva. I don't suppose he'll come to any harm. He has the devil's own luck. Where's my room? *He goes upstairs.*

EVA: Third door at the top. *To Matti*: Now we'll have to sit up in case he starts drinking with the servants and getting familiar with them.

MATTI: That kind of intimacy's always disagreeable. I once worked in a paper mill where the porter gave notice because the director asked him how his son was getting on.

EVA: They all take advantage of my father because of this weakness of his. He's too good.

MATTI: Yes, it's just as well for everyone that he goes on the booze now and again. Then he turns into a good fellow and sees pink rats and wants to stroke them what with being so good.

EVA: I won't have you speaking about your master like that. And I would prefer you not to take the sort of thing he says about the Attaché literally. I would be sorry if you went around repeating what he said in jest.

MATTI: That the Attaché's not a man? What makes a man is a subject about which opinions differ. I used to work for a brewer's wife had a daughter wanted me to come to the bath hut and bring her a dressing-gown because she was so modest. 'Bring my dressing-gown,' she'd say as she stood there stark bollock naked. 'The men keep looking at me as I'm getting into my bath.'

EVA: I don't understand what you are implying.

MATTI: I'm not implying anything. I'm just chatting to help pass the time and keep you amused. When I talk to the gentry I imply nothing and have absolutely no opinions, as those are something they can't abide in servants.

EVA, *after a short pause*: The Attaché is very well thought of in the diplomatic service and set to have an outstanding career; I'd like everyone to be aware of that. He is one of the most promising of its younger members.

MATTI: I see.

EVA: What I was trying to say, when you were standing there just now, was that I didn't find him quite as amusing as my father expected. Naturally what counts isn't whether a man is amusing or not.

MATTI: I knew a gentleman wasn't at all amusing, but it didn't stop him making a million in margarine and fats.

EVA: My engagement was arranged a long time ago. We knew each other as children. It's just that I'm a rather vivacious sort of person and get easily bored.

MATTI: So you're not certain.

EVA: That's not what I said. Look, I don't see why you won't grasp what I am trying to say. Why don't you go to bed?

MATTI: I'm keeping you company.

EVA: There's no need for you to do that. I just wanted to point out that the Attaché is an intelligent and kind-hearted person who ought not to be judged by appearances or by what he says or what he does. He is extremely attentive and anticipates my every wish. He would never perform a vulgar

action or become familiar or try to parade his masculinity.
I have the highest regard for him. Are you feeling sleepy?

MATTI: Just go on talking. I'm only shutting my eyes so's to
concentrate better.

3

Puntila proposes to the early risers

*Early morning in the village. Small wooden houses. One of
them is marked 'Post Office', another 'Veterinary Surgeon', a
third 'Chemist'. In the middle of the square stands a telegraph
pole. Puntila, having run his Studebaker into the pole, is cursing
it.*

PUNTILA: What's happened to the Finnish highway system?
Get out of my way, you rat-shit pole, who are you to block
Puntila's access? Own a forest, got any cows? There, what
did I tell you? Back! If I ring the police and have them arrest
you as a Red I suppose you'll say sorry, but it wasn't you.
He gets out. So you've backed down, and about time too.
*He goes to one of the houses and raps on the window. Sly-
Grog Emma looks out.*

PUNTILA: Good morrow, your ladyship. I trust your ladyship
slept well? I have a trivial request to put to your ladyship.
I am Puntila who farms the manor at Lammi, and I am
severely perturbed because I must somehow obtain legal
alcohol for my seventy fever-ridden cows. Where does the
veterinary surgeon of your village deign to reside? I shall feel
myself regretfully compelled to smash up your dirty little
hovel if you don't show me the way to the vet's.

SLY-GROG EMMA: Heavens, what a state you're in. There's
our vet's house, right there. But did I hear you say you want

alcohol, sir? I have alcohol, good and strong, all my own make.

PUNTILA: Get thee behind me, thou Jezebel! How dare you offer me your illegal liquor? I drink legitimate only, anything else would choke me. Sooner die than fail to respect our law and order, I would. Because everything I do is according to the law. If I want to clobber a man to death I do it within the law or not at all.

SLY-GROG EMMA: Then I hope your legal alcohol makes you sick, sir. *She disappears inside her house. Puntila goes over to the vet's house and rings the bell. The vet looks out.*

PUNTILA: Vet, vet, found you at last. I am Puntila who farms the manor at Lammi, and I've got ninety cows and all ninety have scarlet fever. So I need legal alcohol right away.

THE VET: I fancy you've come to the wrong address; you'd better be on your way, my man.

PUNTILA: Vet, vet, don't disappoint me. You're no true vet or you'd know what they give Puntila throughout the province every time his cows have the scarlet fever. Because I'm not lying to you. If I said they'd got glanders that'd be a lie, but when I tell you they've got scarlet fever that's a delicate hint from one gentleman to another.

THE VET: What happens if I fail to take your hint?

PUNTILA: Then I might tell you that Puntila is the biggest bruiser in the whole of Tavastland province. There's even a folk song about him. He's got three vets on his conscience already. You see what I mean, doctor?

THE VET, *laughing*: Yes, I see all right. If only I could be sure it was scarlet fever . . .

PUNTILA: Look, doctor, if they have red patches – and two of them even have black patches – isn't that scarlet fever in its most virulent form? And what about the headaches they must have when they can't get to sleep, and toss and turn all night long thinking of their sins?

THE VET: Then clearly it is my duty to relieve them.
He throws the prescription down to him.

PUNTILA: And you can send your account to Puntila Hall at Lammi.

Puntila goes to the chemist's and rings the bell hard. While he is waiting there, Sly-Grog Emma comes out of her house.

SLY-GROG EMMA *cleans bottles and sings*:

> In our village one fine morning
> When the plums were ripe and blue
> Came a gig as day was dawning
> Bore a young man passing through.

She goes back into her house. The chemist's assistant looks out of the chemist's shop window.

CHEMIST'S ASSISTANT: You're busting our bell.

PUNTILA: Better bust the bell than wait for ever. Kittikittikittititicktickticktick! What I need is alcohol for ninety cows, my fine plump friend.

CHEMIST'S ASSISTANT: I think what you need is for me to call a policeman.

PUNTILA: Come on, my little sweetheart. Policemen for somebody like Puntila Esquire from Lammi! What good would a single policeman be for him, you'd need at least two. And why policemen anyway, I love the police, they've got bigger feet than anybody else and five toes on each foot because they stand for order and order's what I love. *He gives her the prescription.* Here, my dove, there's law and order for you.

The chemist's assistant goes to get the alcohol. While Puntila is waiting, Sly-Grog Emma again comes out of her house.

SLY-GROG EMMA *sings*:

> As we loaded up our baskets
> Down he lay beneath a tree.
> Fair his head, and if you ask it's
> Not much that he didn't see.

She goes inside her house again. The chemist's assistant brings the alcohol.

CHEMIST'S ASSISTANT, *laughing*: That's a good-sized bottle. I hope you've plenty of herrings for your cows for the morning after. *She hands him the bottle.*

PUNTILA: Glug, glugglug, O music of Finland, loveliest music in the world! My God, I almost forgot. Here am I with alcohol but no girl. And you've no alcohol and no man. Lovely pharmacist, I'd like to get engaged to you.

CHEMIST'S ASSISTANT: Thanks for the honour, Mr Puntila Esquire from Lammi, but I can only get engaged as laid down by law with a ring and a sip of wine.

PUNTILA: Right, so long as you get engaged to me. But get engaged you must, it's high time, for what sort of life do you lead? Tell me what kind of person you are, that's something I should know if I'm going to be engaged to you.

CHEMIST'S ASSISTANT: Me? Here's the sort of life I lead. I did four years at college and now the chemist's charging me for lodging, and paying me less than he pays his cook. Half my wages go to my mother in Tavasthus, she's got a weak heart, passed it on to me. One night in two I can't sleep. The chemist's wife is jealous 'cause the chemist keeps pestering me. The doctor's handwriting's bad, once I got his prescriptions muddled, then I'm always getting stains on my dress from the drugs, and cleaning's so expensive. I've not found a boy friend, the police sergeant and the director of the co-op and the bookseller are all married already. I think I have a very sad life.

PUNTILA: There you are. So – stick to Puntila. Here, have a sip.

CHEMIST'S ASSISTANT: But what about the ring? A ring and a sip of wine, that's what's laid down.

PUNTILA: Haven't you got some curtain rings?

CHEMIST'S ASSISTANT: Do you want one or several?

PUNTILA: Lots, not just one, my girl. Puntila has to have lots of everything. One girl on her own would hardly make any impression on him. You get me?

While the chemist's assistant is fetching a curtain rod, Sly-Grog Emma again comes out of her house.

SLY-GROG EMMA *sings*:

Once the plums were stoned and boiling
He joked condescendingwise
And thereafter, blandly smiling
Stuck his thumb in sundry pies.

The chemist's assistant hands Puntila the rings off the curtain rod.

PUNTILA, *sliding a ring on her finger*: Come up to Puntila Hall on Sunday week. There's to be a big engagement party. *He walks on. Lisu the milkmaid arrives with her pail.* Whoa, my little pigeon, you're the girl I want. Where you off to at this hour?

MILKMAID: Milk the cows.

PUNTILA: What, sitting there with nowt but a bucket between your legs? What sort of life is that? Tell me what sort of life you lead, I'm interested in you.

MILKMAID: Here's the sort of life I lead. Half past three I have to get up, muck out the cowshed and brush down the cows. Then there's the milking to do and after that I wash out the pails with soda and strong stuff that burns your hands. Then more mucking out, and after that I have my coffee but it stinks, it's cheap. I eat my slice of bread and butter and have a bit of shut-eye. In the afternoon I do myself some potatoes and put gravy on them, meat's a thing I never see, with luck the housekeeper'll give me an egg now and again or I might pick one up. Then another lot of mucking out, brushing down, milking and washing out churns. Every day I have to milk twenty-five gallons. Evenings I have bread and milk, they allow me three pints a day for free, but anything else I need to cook I have to buy from the farm. I get one Sunday off in five, but sometimes I go dancing at night and if I make a mistake I'll have a baby. I've got two dresses and I've a bicycle too.

PUNTILA: And I've got a farm and my own flour mill and my own sawmill and no woman. What about it, my little pigeon? Here's the ring and you take a sip from the bottle and it's all according to law. Come up to Puntila Hall on Sunday week, is that a deal?

MILKMAID: It's a deal.

Puntila goes on.

PUNTILA: On, on, let's follow the village street. Fascinating how many of them are already up. They're irresistible at this hour when they've just crept out from under the feathers, when their eyes are still bright and sinful and the world's still young. *He arrives at the telephone exchange. Sandra the telephonist is standing there.*

PUNTILA: Good morning, early bird. Aren't you the well-informed lady who gets all the news from the telephone? Good morning, my dear.

TELEPHONIST: Good morning, Mr Puntila. What are you doing up so early?

PUNTILA: I'm looking for a bride.

TELEPHONIST: Isn't it you I was up half the night ringing around for?

PUNTILA: Yes, there's nothing you don't know. And up half the night all by yourself! I'd like to know what sort of life you lead.

TELEPHONIST: I can tell you that. Here's the sort of life I lead. My pay is fifty marks, but then I haven't been able to leave the switchboard for thirty years. At the back of my house I've got a little potato patch and that's where I get my potatoes from; then I have to pay for fish, and coffee keeps getting dearer. There's nothing goes on in the village or outside it that I don't know; you'd be amazed how much I do. That's why I never got married. I'm secretary of the working men's club, my father was a cobbler. Putting through phone calls, cooking potatoes and knowing everything, that's my life.

PUNTILA: Then it's high time you had a new one. And the quicker the better. Send a wire to the area manager right away to say you're marrying Puntila from Lammi. Here's a ring for you and here's the drink, it's all legal, and you're to come up to Puntila Hall on Sunday week.

TELEPHONIST, *laughing*: I'll be there. I know you're celebrating your daughter's engagement.

PUNTILA, *to Sly-Grog Emma*: And you'll have heard by now, Missis, how I'm getting engaged all round, and I hope you'll be there too.

SLY-GROG EMMA *and the* CHEMIST'S ASSISTANT *sing*:

> Ere the plums were on the table
> Up he jumped and off he ran.
> Ever since we've been unable
> To forget that fair young man.

PUNTILA: And now I shall drive on round the duckpond and through the fir trees and reach the Hiring Fair in good time. Kittikittikittitickticktick! O all you girls of the Tavast country, you who've been getting up so early year after year for nothing, till along comes Puntila and makes it all worth while! Come all of you, come all you dawn stove-lighters and smoke-makers, come barefoot, the fresh grass knows your footsteps and Puntila can hear them!

4

The Hiring Fair

Hiring Fair on the village square at Lammi. Puntila and Matti are looking for farmhands. Fairground music and noise of voices.

PUNTILA: I didn't like the way you let me drive off last night on my own. But as for not sitting up for me, then making me have to drag you out of bed to come here, I call that the bloody limit. It's no better than the disciples on the Mount of Olives, shut up, you've shown me you need watching. You took advantage of my having had a drop too much and thought you could do as you liked.

MATTI: Yes, Mr Puntila.

PUNTILA: I'm not prepared to argue with you, you've hurt me too badly, what I'm telling you's for your own good: be unassuming, that's the way to get on. Start with covetousness and you end in gaol. A servant whose eyes pop out of his head with covetousness at the sight of the gentry eating, for instance, that's something no employer is going to stand for. An unassuming fellow can keep his job, no trouble at all. One knows he's working his arse off, so one winks an eye. But if he's always wanting time off and steaks the size of shithouse seats, then it turns your stomach and you have to get rid of him. I suppose you'd sooner it was the other way round.

MATTI: Yes, Mr Puntila. It said in the 'Helsinki Sanomat' Sunday supplement that being unassuming is a mark of education. Anyone who keeps quiet and controls his passions can go a long way. That fellow Kotilainen who owns the three paper mills outside Viborg is said to be a very unassuming man. Shall we start choosing before all the best ones get snapped up?

PUNTILA: They have to be strong for me. *Looking at a big man.* He's not bad, got the right kind of build. Don't care for his feet, though. Sooner stay sitting on your backside, wouldn't you? *Addressing the shorter man:* How are you at cutting peat?

A FAT MAN: Look, I'm discussing terms with this man.

PUNTILA: So am I. I'd be glad if you didn't interfere.

THE FAT MAN: Who's interfering?

PUNTILA: Don't put impertinent questions to me, I won't

have it. *To a labourer*: At Puntila Hall I pay half a mark per
metre. You can report on Monday. What's your name?

THE FAT MAN: It's an outrage. Here am I, working out how
to house this man and his family, and you stick your oar in.
Some people should be barred from the fair.

PUNTILA: So you've got a family, have you? I can use them
all, the woman can work in the fields, is she strong? How
many children are there? What ages?

THE LABOURER: Three of them. Eight, eleven and twelve.
The eldest's a girl.

PUNTILA: She'll do for the kitchen. You're made to order for
me. *To Matti, so that the fat man can hear*: What do you say
to some people's manners nowadays?

MATTI: I'm speechless.

THE LABOURER: What about lodging?

PUNTILA: You'll lodge like princes, I'll check your references
in the café, get lined up against the wall there. *To Matti*: I'd
take that fellow over there if I went by his build, but his
trousers are too posh for me, he's not going to strain himself.
Clothes are the thing to look out for: too good means he
thinks he's too good to work, too torn means he's got a bad
character. I only need one look to see what he's made of, his
age doesn't matter, if he's old he'll carry as much or more
because he's afraid of being turned off, what I go by is the
man himself. I don't exactly want cripples, but intelligence
is no use to me, that lot spend all day totting up their hours
of work. I don't like that, I'd sooner be on friendly terms
with my men. Must look out for a milkmaid too, don't let
me forget. You find me one or two more hands to choose
from, I got a phone call to make. *Exit to the café.*

MATTI, *addressing a red-headed labourer*: We're looking for
a labourer up at Puntila Hall, for cutting peat. I'm just the
driver, though, 'tain't up to me, the old man's gone to
phone.

THE RED-HEADED MAN: What's it like up at Puntila Hall?

MATTI: So-so. Five pints of milk. Milk's good. You get

potatoes too, I'm told. Room's on the small side.

THE RED-HEADED MAN: How far's school? I've got a little girl.

MATTI: Hour and a quarter.

THE RED-HEADED MAN: That's nothing in fine weather.

MATTI: In summer, you mean.

THE RED-HEADED MAN, *after a pause*: I'd like the job. I've not found anything much, and fair's nearly over.

MATTI: I'll have a word with him. I'll tell him you're unassuming, he's hot on that. That's him now.

PUNTILA, *emerging from the café in a good mood*: Found anything? I got a piglet to take home, cost about twelve marks, mind I don't forget.

MATTI: This one might do. I remembered what you taught me and asked the right questions. He'll darn his trousers, only he hasn't been able to get thread.

PUNTILA: He's good, full of fire. Come to the café, we'll talk it over.

MATTI: It mustn't go wrong, Mr Puntila sir, because the fair will be closing any minute, and he won't find anything else.

PUNTILA: Why should anything go wrong between friends? I rely on your judgement, Matti, that's all right. I know you, think a lot of you. *Indicating a weedy-looking man*: That fellow wouldn't be bad either. I like the look in his eye. I need men for cutting peat, but there's plenty to do in the fields too. Come and talk it over.

MATTI: Mr Puntila, I don't want to speak out of turn, but that man's no use to you, he'll never be able to stand it.

THE WEEDY MAN: Here, I like that. What tells you I'll never be able to stand it?

MATTI: An eleven-hour day in summer. It's just that I don't want to see you let down, Mr Puntila. You'll only have to throw him out when he cracks up or when you see him tomorrow.

PUNTILA: Let's go to the café.

The first labourer, the red-headed one and the weedy man

follow him and Matti to the café, where they all sit down on the bench outside.

PUNTILA: Hey! Coffee! Before we start, there's something I've got to clear up with my friend here. Matti, you must have noticed just now that I was on the verge of one of those attacks of mine I told you about, and I wouldn't have been a bit surprised if you'd clouted me one for speaking to you as I did. Can you forgive me, Matt? I couldn't think of getting down to business if I felt we were on bad terms.

MATTI: That's all under the bridge. Just let it be. These people want their contracts, if you could settle that first.

PUNTILA, *writing something on a slip of paper for the first labourer*: I see, Matti, you're rejecting me. You want to get your own back by being cold and businesslike. *To the labourer*: I've written down what we agreed, including your woman. You'll get milk and flour, and beans in winter.

MATTI: Now give him his earnest-money, or the deal's not valid.

PUNTILA: Don't you rush me. Let me drink my coffee in peace. *To the waitress*: Same again, or why not bring us a big pot and let us serve ourselves? What d'you think of that for a fine strapping girl? I can't stand these hiring fairs. If I want to buy a horse or a cow I'll go to a fair without thinking twice about it. But you're human beings, and it's not right for human beings to be bargained over in a market. Am I right?

THE WEEDY MAN: Absolutely.

MATTI: Excuse me, Mr Puntila, but you're not right. They want work and you've got work, and that's something that has to be bargained over, and whether it's done at a fair or in church it's still buying and selling. And I wish you'd get on with it.

PUNTILA: You're annoyed with me today. That's why you won't admit I'm right when I obviously am. Would you inspect me to see if my feet are crooked, the way you inspect a horse's teeth?

MATTI, *laughs*: No, I'd take you on trust. *Referring to the red-*

headed man: He's got a missus, but his little girl's still at school.

PUNTILA: Is she nice? There's the fat man again. It's fellows like him behaving that way that makes bad blood among the workers, acting the boss and all. I bet he's in the National Guard and has his men out on Sundays training to beat the Russians. What do you people say?

THE RED-HEADED MAN: My wife could do washing. She gets through more in five hours than most women in ten.

PUNTILA: Matt, I can see it isn't all forgiven and forgotten between us. Tell them your story about the ghosts, that'll give them something to laugh about.

MATTI: Later. Do get on and pay them their earnest-money. It's getting late, I tell you. You're holding everyone up.

PUNTILA, *drinking*: I'm not going to. I won't be jockeyed into being so inhuman. I want to get on terms with my men first, before we all commit ourselves. I must start by telling them what kind of fellow I am so they can see if they're going to get on with me or not. That's the question: what kind of fellow am I?

MATTI: Mr Puntila, none of them's interested in that; they're interested in their contract. I'm recommending that one [*pointing to the red-headed man*] he may do all right for you, at any rate you can find out. And *you*'d do better to look for a different job, I'd say. You'll never earn your keep on the land.

PUNTILA: Isn't that Surkkala over there? What's Surkkala doing at a hiring fair?

MATTI: He's looking for a job. Don't you remember you promised the parson you'd get rid of him because they say he's a Red?

PUNTILA: What, Surkkala? The one intelligent worker on the whole estate? Give him ten marks at once, tell him to come along and we'll take him back in the Studebaker, we can strap his bicycle on the luggage carrier and no nonsense about going anywhere else. Four children he's got too, what must he think of me? Parson be buggered, I'll forbid him the house for his inhumanity. Surkkala's a first-class worker.

MATTI: There's no hurry, he won't find jobs easy to get with his reputation. I'd just like to settle this lot first. I don't believe you're serious about it, you're simply having a lark.

PUNTILA, *with a pained smile*: So that's what you think of me, Matti. You don't understand me, do you, though I've given you every chance to.

THE RED-HEADED MAN: Do you mind writing out my contract now. Or I'll have to look for something else.

PUNTILA: You're frightening them away, Matt. Your high-handed behaviour forces me to deny my real self. But that's not me, let me show you. I don't go buying people up, I give them a home on the Puntila estate. Don't I?

THE RED-HEADED MAN: Then I'm off. I need a job. *He goes.*

PUNTILA: Stop! He's gone. I could have used him. His trousers wouldn't matter. I look deeper than that. I don't like fixing a deal after drinking just one glass, how can you do business when you'd rather be singing because life's so beautiful? When I start thinking about that drive home – I find the Hall looks its best in the evenings, on account of the birch trees – we must have another drink. Here, buy yourselves a round, have a good time with Puntila, I like to see it and I don't count the cost when it's with people I like. *He quickly gives a mark to each of them. To the weedy man*: Don't be put off by him, he's got something against me, you'll be able to stand it all right. I'll put you in the mill, in a cushy job.

MATTI: Why not make him out a contract?

PUNTILA: What for, now we know each other? I give you people my word it'll be all right. You understand what that means, the word of a Tavastland farmer? Mount Hatelma can crumble, it's not very likely but it can, Tavasthus Castle can collapse, why not, but the word of a Tavastland farmer stands for ever, everyone knows that. You can come along.

THE WEEDY MAN: Thank you very much, Mr Puntila, I'll

certainly come.

MATTI: You'd do better to get the hell out of here. I'm not blaming you, Mr Puntila, I'm only worried for the men's sake.

PUNTILA, *warmly*: That's what I wanted to hear, Matti. I knew you weren't the sort to bear a grudge. And I admire your integrity, and how you always have my best interests at heart. But it is Puntila's privilege to have his own worst interests at heart, that's something you haven't yet learnt. All the same, Matt, you mustn't stop saying what you think. Promise me you won't. *To the others*: At Tammerfors he lost his job with a company director because when the man drove he so crashed the gears that Matt told him he ought to have been a public hangman.

MATTI: That was a stupid thing to do.

PUNTILA, *seriously*: It's those stupid things that make me respect you.

MATTI, *getting up*: Then let's go. And what about Surkkala?

PUNTILA: Matti, Matti, O thou of little faith! Didn't I tell you we'd take him back with us because he's a first-rate worker and a man who thinks for himself? And that reminds me, the fat man just now who wanted to get my men away from me. I've one or two things to say to him, he's a typical capitalist.

5

Scandal at Puntila Hall

Yard at Puntila Hall, with a bath hut into which we can see. Morning. Above the main entrance to the house Laina the cook and Fina the parlourmaid are nailing a sign saying 'Welcome to the engagement party'. Through the gateway come Puntila and Matti with a number of woodcutters including Red Surkkala.

LAINA: Welcome back to Puntila Hall. Miss Eva's here with the Attaché and his honour the Judge, and they're all having breakfast.

PUNTILA: First thing I want to do is apologise to you and your family, Surkkala. May I ask you to go and get your children, all four of them, so I can express my personal regret for the fear and insecurity they must have been through?

SURKKALA: No call for that, Mr Puntila.

PUNTILA, *seriously*: Oh yes there is.

Surkkala goes.

PUNTILA: These gentlemen are staying. Get them all an aquavit, Laina. I'm taking them on to work in the forest.

LAINA: I thought you were selling the forest.

PUNTILA: Me? I'm not selling any forest. My daughter's got her dowry between her legs, right?

MATTI: So maybe we could settle their contracts, Mr Puntila, and then you'll have it off your chest.

PUNTILA: I'm going into the sauna, Fina; bring aquavits for the gentlemen and a coffee for me.

He goes into the sauna.

THE WEEDY MAN: Think he'll take me on?

MATTI: Not when he's sober and has a look at you.

THE WEEDY MAN: But when he's drunk he won't settle any contracts.

MATTI: I told you people it was a mistake coming up here till you had your contracts in your hands.

Fina brings out aquavit, and each of the labourers takes a glass.

THE LABOURER: What's he like otherwise?

MATTI: Too familiar. It won't matter to you, you'll be in the forest, but I'm with him in the car, I can't get away from him and before I know where I am he's turning all human on me. I'll have to give notice.

Surkkala comes back with his four children. The eldest girl is holding the baby.

MATTI, *quietly*: For God's sake clear off right away. Once he's had his bath and knocked back his coffee he'll be stone cold sober and better look out if he catches you around the yard. Take my advice, you'll keep out of his sight the next day or two.

Surkkala nods and is about to hasten away with the children.

PUNTILA, *who has undressed and listened but failed to hear the end of this, peers out of the bath hut and observes Surkkala and the children*: I'll be with you in a moment. Matti, come inside, I need you to pour the water over me. *To the weedy man*: You can come in too, I want to get to know you better. *Matti and the weedy man follow Puntila into the bath hut. Matti sloshes water over Puntila. Surkkala quickly goes off with the children.*

PUNTILA: One bucket's enough. I loathe water.

MATTI: You'll have to bear with a few buckets more, then you can have a coffee and be the perfect host.

PUNTILA: I can be the perfect host as I am. You're just wanting to bully me.

THE WEEDY MAN: I say that's enough too. Mr Puntila can't stand water, it's obvious.

PUNTILA: There you are, Matti, there speaks somebody who feels for me. I'd like you to tell him how I saw off the fat man at the hiring fair.

Enter Fina.

PUNTILA: Here's that golden creature with my coffee. Is it strong? I'd like a liqueur with it.

MATTI: Then what's the point of the coffee? No liqueur for you.

PUNTILA: I know, you're cross with me for keeping these people waiting, and quite right too. But tell them about the fat man. Fina must hear this. *Starts telling*: One of those nasty fat individuals with a blotchy face, a proper capitalist, who was trying to sneak a worker away from me. I grabbed hold of him, but when we reached my car he'd got his gig parked alongside it. You go on, Matt, I must drink my coffee.

MATTI: He was livid when he saw Mr Puntila, and took his whip and lashed his pony till it reared.

PUNTILA: I can't abide cruelty to animals.

MATTI: Mr Puntila took the pony by the reins and calmed it down and told the fat man what he thought of him, and I thought he was going to get a crack with the whip, only the fat man didn't dare since we outnumbered him. So he muttered something about uneducated people, thinking we wouldn't hear it perhaps, but Mr Puntila's got a sharp ear when he dislikes someone and answered back at once: had he been educated well enough to know that being too fat can give you a stroke?

PUNTILA: Tell him how he went red as a turkeycock and got so angry he couldn't make a witty comeback in front of them all.

MATTI: He went as red as a turkeycock and Mr Puntila told him he shouldn't get excited, it was bad for him on account of his unhealthy corpulence. He ought never to go red in the face, it was a sign the blood was going to his brain, and for the sake of his loved ones he should avoid that.

PUNTILA: You're forgetting I addressed most of my remarks to you, saying we shouldn't be exciting him and ought to treat him gently. That got under his skin, did you notice?

MATTI: We spoke about him as if he wasn't there, everybody laughed more and more and he kept getting redder and redder. That was when he really started looking like a turkeycock, before that he was more a sort of faded brick. He asked for it; what did he have to lash his horse for? I remember a fellow once got so cross when a ticket fell out of his hatband where he'd stuck it for safekeeping that he trampled his hat flat underfoot in a chock-full third class compartment.

PUNTILA: You're losing the thread. I went on and told him that any violent physical exercise like lashing ponies with a whip could easily kill him. That in itself was good enough reason why he shouldn't maltreat his beast, not in his condition.

FINA: Nobody should.

PUNTILA: That earns you a liqueur, Fina. Go and help yourself.

MATTI: She's holding the coffee tray. I hope you're starting to feel better now, Mr Puntila?

PUNTILA: I feel worse.

MATTI: I thought it was really fine of Mr Puntila to tell that fellow where he got off. Because he could easily have said 'What business is it of mine? I'm not making enemies among the neighbours.'

PUNTILA, *who is gradually sobering up*: I'm not afraid of enemies.

MATTI: That's true. But there aren't many people who can say that. You can. And you can always send your mares somewhere else.

PUNTILA: Why should we send the mares somewhere else?

MATTI: They were saying afterwards that that fat bloke is the one who has bought Summala, which has the only stallion within five hundred miles who's any good for our mares.

FINA: Gosh, it was the new owner of Summala. And you only found that out afterwards?

Puntila gets up and goes behind to pour a further bucket of water over his head.

MATTI: Not afterwards, actually. Mr Puntila already knew. He yelled after the fat man that his stallion was too beaten up for our mares. How did you put it?

PUNTILA, *curtly*: Somehow.

MATTI: Not somehow. It was witty.

FINA: But what a job it will be if we have to send the mares all that distance to be served.

PUNTILA, *brooding*: More coffee. *He is given it.*

MATTI: Kindness to animals is supposed to be a great thing with the Tavast people. That's what so surprised me about the fat man. Another thing I heard later was that he was Mrs Klinckmann's brother-in-law. I bet if Mr Puntila had known that he'd have given him an even worse going-over.

Puntila gives him a look.

FINA: Coffeee strong enough, was it?

PUNTILA: Don't ask stupid questions. You can see I've drunk it, can't you? *To Matti*: You, don't just sit on your bottom, stop loafing, clean some boots, wash the car. Don't contradict, and if I catch you spreading malicious rumours I'll put it down in your reference, so watch out.

Exit in his bathrobe, brooding.

FINA: What did you want to let him make that scene with the fat owner of Summala for?

MATTI: Am I his guardian angel? Look, if I see him doing a dangerous and kindly action, stupidly because it's against his own interests, am I supposed to stop him? Anyhow I couldn't. When he's pissed as that he's got real fire in him. He'd just despise me, and I don't want him to despise me when he's pissed.

PUNTILA *off, calls*: Fina!

Fina follows with his clothes.

PUNTILA, *to Fina*: Now this is what I've decided, and I want you to listen so what I say doesn't get twisted around later as it usually does. *Indicating one of the labourers*: I'd have taken that one, he isn't out to curry favour, he wants to work, but I've thought it over and I'm taking nobody at all. I'm going to sell the forest in any case, and you can blame it on Kim there for deliberately leaving me in the dark about something I needed to know, the bastard. And that reminds me. *Calls*: Here, you! *Matti emerges from the bath hut.* Yes, you. Give me your jacket. You're to hand over your jacket, d'you hear? *He is handed Matti's jacket.* Got you, boyo. *Shows him the wallet.* That's what I found in your pocket. Had a feeling about you, spotted you for an old lag first go off. Is that my wallet or isn't it?

MATTI: Yes, Mr Puntila.

PUNTILA: Now you're for it, ten years' gaol, all I have to do is ring the police.

MATTI: Yes, Mr Puntila.

PUNTILA: But that's a favour I'm not doing you. So you can lead the life of Riley in a cell, lying around and eating the taxpayer's bread, what? That'd suit you down to the ground. At harvest time too. So you'd get out of driving the tractor. But I'm putting it all down in your reference, you get me?

MATTI: Yes, Mr Puntila.

Puntila walks angrily towards the house. On the threshold stands Eva, carrying her straw hat. She has been listening.

THE WEEDY MAN: Should I come along then, Mr Puntila?

PUNTILA: You're no use to me whatever, you'll never stand it.

THE WEEDY MAN: But the hiring fair's over now.

PUNTILA: You should have thought of that sooner instead of trying to take advantage of my friendly mood. I remember exactly who takes advantage of it. *He goes brooding into the house.*

THE LABOURER: That's them. Bring you here in their car, and now we have to walk the six miles back on our flat feet. And no job. That's what comes of letting yourself get taken in by their acting friendly.

THE WEEDY MAN: I'll report him.

MATTI: Who to?

Embittered, the labourers leave the yard.

EVA: But why don't you stick up for yourself? We all know he hands his wallet to somebody else to pay for him when he's been drinking.

MATTI: If I stuck up for myself he wouldn't understand. I've noticed that the gentry don't much like it when you stick up for yourself.

EVA: Don't act so innocent and humble. I'm not in the mood for jokes today.

MATTI: Yes, they're hitching you to the Attaché.

EVA: Don't be crude. The Attaché is a very sweet person, only not to get married to.

MATTI: That's normal enough. No girl's going to be able to marry all the sweet people or all the Attachés, she has to settle for a particular one.

EVA: My father's leaving it entirely up to me, you heard him say so, that's why he said I could marry you if I liked. Only he has promised my hand to the Attaché and doesn't want anyone to say he doesn't keep his word. That's the only reason why I'm taking so long to make up my mind and might accept him after all.

MATTI: Got yourself in a nice jam, you have.

EVA: I am not in any jam, as you so vulgarly put it. In fact I can't think why I'm discussing such intimate matters with you.

MATTI: It's a very human habit, discussing. It's one great advantage we have over the animals. If cows could discuss, for instance, there'd soon be no more slaughterhouses.

EVA: What has that to do with my saying I don't think I shall be happy with the Attaché? And that he must be the one to back out, only how's one to suggest it to him?

MATTI: That's not the sort of thing you can do with a pinprick, it needs a sledgehammer.

EVA: What d'you mean?

MATTI: I mean that it's a job for me. I'm crude.

EVA: How might you picture helping me in such a delicate situation?

MATTI: Well, suppose I'd felt encouraged by Mr Puntila's kind suggestion that you should take me, like he let slip when plastered. And you felt the lure of my crude strength, just think of Tarzan, and the Attaché caught us and said to himself, she's unworthy of me, messing around with the chauffeur.

EVA: That'd be too much to ask of you.

MATTI: It'd be part of the job, like cleaning the car. It needn't take above a quarter of an hour. All we need do is show him we are on terms of intimacy.

EVA: And how do you propose to show him that?

MATTI: I could call you by your Christian name in his presence.

EVA: For instance?

MATTI: Your blouse has a button undone, Eva.

EVA *feels behind her*: No, it hasn't; oh, I see, you'd started acting. But he wouldn't mind. He's not all that easily offended, he's too much in debt for that.

MATTI: Or I could accidentally pull one of your stockings out of my pocket when I blow my nose, and make sure that he sees.

EVA: That's a bit better, but then he'll only say you pinched it in my absence because you have a secret crush on me. *Pause*. You've not got a bad imagination for that sort of thing, it seems.

MATTI: I do what I can, Miss Eva. I'm trying to picture every conceivable situation and awkward occasion that might involve us both, and hoping to come up with the right answer.

EVA: You can stop that.

MATTI: All right, I'll stop it.

EVA: For instance, what?

MATTI: If his debts are all that enormous then we'll simply have to come out of the bath hut together, nothing less will do the trick, he'll always manage to find some sort of innocent explanation. For instance if I merely kiss you he'd say I was forcing myself on you 'cause your beauty overcame me. And so on.

EVA: I never can tell when you're just laughing at me behind my back. One can't be sure with you.

MATTI: What do you want to be sure for? You're not making an investment, are you? Being unsure is much more human, as your daddy would say. I like women to be unsure.

EVA: Yes, I can imagine that.

MATTI: There you are, your imagination's not so bad either.

EVA: I was only saying how difficult it is to tell what you're really up to.

MATTI: That's something you can't tell with a dentist either, what he'll be up to once you're sitting in his chair.

EVA: Look, when you talk that way I realise the bath hut business wouldn't work, because you'd be sure to take advantage of the situation.

MATTI: At least something's sure now. If you're going to hesitate much longer I shall lose all desire to compromise you, Miss Eva.

EVA: Much better if you do it with no particular desire. Now listen to me. I accept the bath hut idea, I trust you. They'll be through with breakfast any minute, after which they're bound to walk up and down the verandah to discuss the engagement. We'd better go in there right away.

MATTI: You go ahead, I'll just fetch a pack of cards.

EVA: What d'you want cards for?

MATTI: How d'you think we're going to pass the time?

He goes into the house; she slowly walks towards the bath hut. Laina the cook arrives with a basket.

LAINA: Good morning, Miss Eva, I'm off to pick cucumbers. Would you like to come too?

EVA: No, I've a slight headache and I feel like a bath.

She goes in. Laina stands shaking her head. Puntila and the Attaché come out of the house smoking cigars.

THE ATTACHÉ: Puntila, old man, I think I'll drive Eva down to Monte and see if I can borrow Baron Vaurien's Rolls. It would be a good advertisement for Finland and her foreign service. You've no idea how few presentable ladies we have in our diplomatic corps.

PUNTILA *to Laina*: Where's my daughter? She went out.

LAINA: She's in the bath hut, Mr Puntila, she had such a headache and felt she needed a bath. *Exit.*

PUNTILA: She often gets these moods. First time I ever heard of anyone bathing with a headache.

THE ATTACHÉ: What an original idea; but you know, my dear fellow, we don't make nearly enough of the Finnish sauna. That's what I told the permanent secretary when there was some question of our raising a loan. Finnish culture is being put over all wrong. Why is there no sauna in Whitehall?

PUNTILA: What I want to know from you is if your minister's really coming to Puntila Hall for the engagement party.

THE ATTACHÉ: He definitely accepted. He owes me that, because I introduced him to the Lehtinens, the Commercial Bank chappie, he's interested in nickel.

PUNTILA: I want a word with him.

THE ATTACHÉ: He's got a soft spot for me, so they all say at the Ministry. He told me, 'We could post you anywhere, you'll never do anything indiscreet, politics don't interest you.' He thinks I'm a good advertisement for the service.

PUNTILA: You're a bright fellow, Eino. It'll be amazing if you don't do well in your career; but mind you take that seriously about the minister coming. I insist on that, it'll give me an idea what they think of you.

THE ATTACHÉ: Puntila, I'm sure as eggs is eggs. I'm always lucky. In our ministry it's become proverbial. If I lose something it comes back to me, dead sure.

Matti arrives with a towel over his shoulder and goes to the bath hut.

PUNTILA, *to Matti*: What are you hanging around for, my man? I'd be ashamed to loaf about like that. I'd ask myself what I was doing to earn my pay. You'll get no reference from me. You can rot like a putrid oyster nobody will eat.

MATTI: Yes, Mr Puntila, sir.

Puntila turns back to the Attaché. Matti calmly walks into the bath hut. At first Puntila thinks nothing of it, then it suddenly strikes him that Eva must be in there too, and he gazes after Matti in astonishment.

PUNTILA, *to the Attaché*: What kind of terms are you on with Eva?

THE ATTACHÉ: Good terms. She is a little chilly to me, but then that is her nature. It is not unlike our position with regard to Russia. In diplomatic parlance we'd say relations are correct. Come along, I think I'll pick Eva a bunch of white roses, don't you know.

PUNTILA *walks off with him, glancing at the bath hut*: A very sensible thing to do, I'd say.

MATTI, *inside the hut*: They saw me come in. All according to plan.

EVA: I'm amazed my father didn't stop you. The cook told him I was in here.

MATTI: He didn't catch on till too late, he must have a terrible hangover today. And it would have been bad timing, too early, because it's not enough to want to compromise someone, something has got to have happened.

EVA: I don't think they're going to get dirty thoughts at all. In the middle of the morning it means nothing.

MATTI: That's what you think. It's a sign of exceptional passion. Five hundred rummy? *He deals.* I had a boss once in Viborg could eat any time day or night. In the middle of the afternoon, just before tea, he made them roast him a chicken. Eating was a passion with him. He was in the government.

EVA: How can you compare the two things?

MATTI: Why not? Like with love, you get people are dead set on it. You to play. D'you imagine the cows always wait till night-time? It's summer now, you feel in the mood. So in you pop to the bath hut. Phew, it's hot. *Takes off his jacket.* Why don't you take something off? My seeing won't hurt. Half a pfennig a point, I'd suggest.

EVA: I've an idea what you're saying is rather vulgar. Kindly don't treat me as if I were a milkmaid.

MATTI: I've nothing against milkmaids.

EVA: You've no sense of respect.

MATTI: I'm always being told that. Drivers are known to be particularly awkward individuals without any esteem for the upper crust. That's because we hear what the upper crust are saying to one another on the back seat. I've got a hundred and forty, what about you?

EVA: When I was at my convent in Brussels I never heard anything but decent talk.

MATTI: I'm not talking about decent or indecent, I'm talking

about stupid. Your deal, but cut first to be on the safe side.
Puntila and the Attaché return. The latter is carrying a bunch of roses.

THE ATTACHÉ: She's so witty. I said to her 'You know, you'd be perfect if you weren't so rich'; and she said after barely a moment's thought, 'But I rather like being rich.' Hahaha! And d'you know, Puntila old man, that's exactly the answer I had from Mademoiselle Rothschild when Baroness Vaurien introduced us. She's very witty too.

MATTI: You must giggle as if I'm tickling you, or else they'll walk brazenly past. *Eva giggles a bit over her cards.* Try to sound more as if it was fun.

THE ATTACHÉ, *stopping*: Wasn't that Eva?

PUNTILA: Certainly not, it must be somebody else.

MATTI, *loudly, over the cards*: Ee, aren't you ticklish!

THE ATTACHÉ: What's that?

MATTI, *quietly*: Put up a bit of a fight.

PUNTILA: That's my chauffeur in the bath hut. Why don't you take your bouquet into the house?

EVA, *acting, loudly*: No! Don't!

MATTI: Oh yes, I will!

THE ATTACHÉ: You know, Puntila, that did sound awfully like Eva.

PUNTILA: Do you mind not being offensive?

MATTI: Now for some endearments and abandon your vain resistance!

EVA: No! No! No! *Softly*: What do I say now?

MATTI: Tell me I mustn't. Can't you get into the spirit of it? Bags of lust.

EVA: Sweetheart, you mustn't.

PUNTILA *thunders*: Eva!

MATTI: Go on, go on, unbridled passion! *He clears away the cards while they continue to suggest the love scene.* If he comes in we'll have to get down to it, like it or not.

EVA: That's out of the question.

MATTI, *kicking over a bench*: Then out you go, but like a

drowned spaniel!

PUNTILA: Eva!

Matti carefully runs his hand through Eva's hair to disarrange it, while she undoes one of her top blouse buttons. Then she steps out.

EVA: Did you call, Daddy? I was just going to change and have a swim.

PUNTILA: What the devil are you up to, messing about in the bath hut? D'you imagine we're stone deaf?

THE ATTACHÉ: No need to fly off the handle, Puntila. Why shouldn't Eva use the bath hut?

Out comes Matti and stands behind Eva.

EVA, *slightly cowed, without noticing Matti*: What do you imagine you heard, daddy? It was nothing.

PUNTILA: Is that what you call nothing, then? Perhaps you'll turn round and look.

MATTI, *pretending to be embarrassed*: Mr Puntila, Miss Eva and I were just having a game of five hundred rummy. Look at the cards if you don't believe me. You're putting a wrong interpretation on it.

PUNTILA: Shut up, you. You're fired. *To Eva*: What's Eino supposed to think?

THE ATTACHÉ: Y'know, old boy, if they were playing five hundred rummy you must have got it wrong. Princess Bibesco once got so excited over baccarat her pearl necklace broke. I've brought you some white roses, Eva. *He gives her the roses.* Come on, Puntila, what about a game of billiards? *He tugs him away by the sleeve.*

PUNTILA *growls*: I'll be talking to you later, Eva. As for you, trash, if I once hear you so much as say bo to my daughter instead of snatching your filthy cap off your head and standing to attention and feeling embarrassed because you haven't washed behind your ears – shut up, will you? – then you can pack your stinking socks and go. You should look up to your employer's daughter as to a higher being that has graciously condescended to come down amongst us. Leave

me alone, Eino, d'you think I can tolerate this sort of thing?
To Matti: Repeat that: what should you do?

MATTI: Look up to her as to a higher being that has graciously
condescended to come down amongst us, Mr Puntila.

PUNTILA: You open your eyes wide in incredulous
amazement at such a rare sight, you trash.

MATTI: I open my eyes wide in incredulous amazement, Mr
Puntila.

PUNTILA: Blushing like a lobster because well before your
confirmation you were having impure thoughts about
women, at the sight of such a model of innocence, and
wishing the earth would come and swallow you up, get me?

MATTI: I get you.

The Attaché drags Puntila off into the house.

EVA: Washout.

MATTI: His debts are even bigger than we thought.

6

A conversation about crayfish

*Farm kitchen at Puntila Hall. Evening. Intermittent dance
music from outside. Matti is reading the paper.*

FINA, *entering*: Miss Eva'd like a word with you.

MATTI: All right. I'll just finish my coffee.

FINA: No need to impress me by drinking it in such a languid
way. I bet you're getting ideas on account of Miss Eva taking
a bit of notice of you now and then whenever there's no
society for her on the estate and she needs to see someone.

MATTI: Evenings like this I quite enjoy getting ideas. Like
supposing you, Fina, felt like having a look at the river with

me, then I won't have heard Miss Eva wants me and I'll come with you.

FINA: Don't really feel like it.

MATTI, *picking up a paper*: Thinking about the school-teacher?

FINA: There's been nothing between me and the schoolteacher. He was friendly and wanted to educate me by lending me a book.

MATTI: Too bad he gets such rotten pay for his education. I get 300 marks and a schoolteacher gets 200, but then I have to be better at my job. You see, if a schoolteacher's no good then it only means the local people never learn to read the newspapers. In the old days that would have been a retrograde step, but what's the use of reading the papers now, when the censorship leaves nothing in them? I'd go so far as to say that if they did away with schoolteachers altogether then they wouldn't need censorship either, which'd save the state what it pays the censors. But if I have a breakdown on a class 3 road then the gentry are forced to plod through the mud and fall in the ditch 'cause they're all pissed.

Matti beckons to Fina and she sits on his knee. Judge and Lawyer appear with towels over their shoulders, returning from their steam bath.

THE JUDGE: Haven't you anything to drink, some of that marvellous buttermilk you used to have here?

MATTI: Would you like the parlourmaid to bring it?

THE JUDGE: No, just show us where it's kept.

Matti serves them with a ladle. Exit Fina.

THE LAWYER: That's great stuff.

THE JUDGE: I always have that after my shower at Puntila's.

THE LAWYER: These Finnish summer nights!

THE JUDGE: They make a lot of work for me. All those paternity cases are a great tribute to the Finnish summer night. The courthouse brings it home to you what a nice place a birch wood is, as for the river they can't go near it without going weak all over. One woman up before me blamed the hay, said it smelt so strong. Picking berries is a bad mistake and milking the cows brings its penalties. Each bush by the roadside needs to be surrounded with barbed wire. In the baths they separate the sexes, or else the temptation would be too great, then afterwards they go strolling across the meadows together. It's just impossible to stop them in summer. If they're on bicycles they jump off them, if there's a hayloft they climb in it; in the kitchen it happens because of the heat, and in the open because there's a cool wind. Half the time they're making babies 'cause the summer's so short, and the other half 'cause the winter's so long.

THE LAWYER: What I like is the way the old people are allowed to take part too. I'm thinking of the witnesses that come along. They see it. They see the couple disappearing into the coppice, they see the clogs on the barn floor and how hot the girl looks when she gets back from picking bilberries, which is something nobody gets all that hot over 'cause nobody works all that hard at it. And they don't just see, they hear. Milk churns rattle, bedsteads creak. That way they join in with their eyes and ears and get something out of the summer.

THE JUDGE, *since there is a ring on the bell, to Matti*: Perhaps you'd go and see what it is they want? Or we could always tell them that the eight-hour day is being taken seriously out here.

Exit with the lawyer. Matti has sat down to read his paper once more.

EVA *enters with an ultra-long cigarette holder and a seductive walk picked up from the films*: I rang for you. Is there anything more you have to do here?

MATTI: No, I'm not on again till six a.m.

EVA: I wondered if you'd like to row over to the island with me and catch a few crayfish for my engagement party tomorrow.

MATTI: Isn't it about time for bed?

EVA: I'm not a bit tired. I don't seem to sleep very well in the summer, I don't know why. Could you go off to sleep if you went to bed right now?

MATTI: Yes.

EVA: I envy you. Will you get out the nets, then? My father has expressed a desire for crayfish. *She turns on her heel and starts to leave, again showing off the walk picked up from the cinema.*

MATTI, *changing his mind*: I think I'll come after all. I'll row you.

EVA: Aren't you too tired?

MATTI: I've woken up and feel fine now. Only you'd better get changed into something you can go wading in.

EVA: The nets are in the pantry. *Exit.*
Matti puts on his jacket.

EVA, *reappearing in very short shorts*: But you haven't got the nets out.

MATTI: We'll catch them in our hands. It's much nicer. I'll show you how.

EVA: But it's easier with nets.

MATTI: The other day Cook and I and the parlourmaid were over on the island and we did it with our hands and it was very nice, you ask them. I'm pretty nippy. How about you? Lots of folk are all thumbs. Of course the crayfish move quick and it's slippery on the rocks, but it's quite light out, just a few clouds, I had a look.

EVA, *hesitating*: I'd sooner we used the nets. We'll catch more.

MATTI: Have we got to have such a lot?

EVA: Father won't eat anything unless there's lots of it.

MATTI: That's bad. I thought we could catch one or two, then have a bit of a talk. It's a nice night.

EVA: Don't keep saying everything's nice. You'd do better to get out the nets.

MATTI: Why d'you have to be so serious and bloodthirsty about the poor old crayfish? If we fill a couple of bags it ought to do. I know a place where there are lots of them; five minutes' work and we'd have enough to convince anybody.

EVA: What do you mean by that? Are you in the least interested in catching crayfish?

MATTI *after a pause*: Perhaps it is a bit late. I got to be up at six and take the Studebaker down to the station to collect the Attaché. If we're mucking about on the island till three or four there won't be much time left for sleep. Of course I could row you over if you're dead set on it.

Eva turns without a word and goes out. Matti takes off his jacket and sits down with his paper. Enter Laina from the bath.

LAINA: Fina and the milkmaid are asking if you don't feel like coming down to the lake. They're having some fun there.

MATTI: I'm tired. I was over at the hiring fair, then before that I had to take the tractor out on the heath and both the tow-ropes broke.

LAINA: Same here. All this baking's fair killed me. I've no use for engagements. But I had to tear myself away to come to bed, I really did, it's so light still and a shame to waste time sleeping. *Looks out of the window as she leaves.* I might just go back for a bit, the groom's got his harmonica out and I like that. *Exit dead tired but still dogged.*

EVA *enters*: I want you to take me to the station.

MATTI: It'll take me five minutes to bring the car round. I'll wait at the front door.

EVA: Good. I notice you don't ask me what I'm going for.

MATTI: I'd say you were thinking of catching the 11.10 to Helsinki.

EVA: Anyway that doesn't surprise you, I see.

MATTI: What d'you mean, surprise? It changes nothing and leads to very little when chauffeurs are surprised. It's seldom noticed and has no significance.

EVA: I'm going to Brussels for a few weeks to stay with a girlfriend, and I don't want to bother my father about it. You'll have to lend me 200 marks for my ticket. My father will pay it back as soon as I write.

MATTI *unenthusiastic*: I see.

EVA: I hope you aren't anxious about the money. Even if my father doesn't care who I get engaged to he wouldn't particularly want to be indebted to you.

MATTI *cautiously*: Suppose I let you have it, I'm not sure he would feel all that indebted.

EVA *after a pause*: Please forgive me for having asked you.

MATTI: I'd have thought your father would care all right if you go off in the middle of the night just before your engagement party, when the dinner's in the oven, so to speak. He may have said unthinking-like that you could make do with me, but you mustn't hold that against him. Your father's acting all for your best, Miss Eva. He told me as much. When he's pissed – I mean when he's had a glass or two more than he should – then he's not clear what your best is, he just goes by instinct. But once he's sobered up he's a very intelligent man again and buys you an Attaché who's value for money, and you become Ambassadress in Paris or Estonia or somewhere and can do as you please if you feel like something on a fine evening, and if you don't you won't have to.

EVA: So now you're saying I ought to take Mr Silakka?

MATTI: Miss Eva, you're not in a financial position to upset your father.

EVA: I see, you've changed your mind, you're just a weathercock.

MATTI: That's right. Except that it's not fair to talk about weathercocks; it's thoughtless. They're made of iron, solid as can be, only they haven't got the firm base would let them take a proper stand. Me too, I haven't got the base.

He rubs thumb and forefinger together.

EVA: That means I'll have to be careful about taking your advice, if I can't have honest advice because your base is lacking. Your beautiful speech about my father having my best interests at heart boils down to the fact that you don't care to risk the money for my ticket.

MATTI: And my job too, it's not a bad one.

EVA: You're quite a materialist, aren't you, Mr Altonen? Or as they might say in your world, you know which side your bread's buttered. Anyway I've never heard anybody admit so openly how much he minds about his money and his own welfare in general. It's not only the rich who spend their time thinking about money, I see.

MATTI: I'm sorry to have disappointed you. Can't be helped, though, since you asked me straight out. If you'd just given a hint or two and left it hanging in the air, between the lines, so to speak, then we wouldn't have had to mention money at all. It always strikes a discordant note.

EVA *sitting down*: I am not marrying the Attaché.

MATTI: I been thinking, and it puzzles me why you pick on him not to get married to. The whole lot of them seem alike to me, and I've had to handle plenty in my time. They been to posh schools and they don't throw their boots at you, not even when they're drunk, and they're not tight with their money, specially when it isn't theirs, and they appreciate you just the same way they tell one bottle of wine from another, because they been taught.

EVA: I'm not having the Attaché. I think I'll have you.

MATTI: How come?

EVA: My father could give us a sawmill.

MATTI: Give you, you mean.

EVA: Us, if we get married.

MATTI: I once worked on an estate in Karelia where the boss had been a farmhand. The lady of the house used to pack him off fishing whenever parson called. Other times when there was company he would sit in the corner by the stove playing patience by himself; soon as he'd opened the bottles, that is. The kids were quite big by then. They called him by his Christian name: 'Victor, fetch my gumboots, get a move on, will you?' I wouldn't care for that sort of thing, Miss Eva.

EVA: No, you'd want to be the master. I can picture how you'd treat a woman.

MATTI: Been thinking about it?

EVA: Of course not. I suppose you imagine I've got nothing to do all day but think about you. I don't know where you get such ideas from. Anyway I'm sick of hearing you talk about nothing but yourself the whole time, and what you'd care for and what you've heard, and don't think I don't see through all your innocent stories and your impertinences. I just can't stand the sight of you any longer, and I hate egoists, I hate them! *Exit. Matti once more sits down with his paper.*

7

The confederation of Mr Puntila's fiancées

Yard at Puntila Hall. It is Sunday morning. On the verandah Puntila is heard arguing with Eva as he shaves. Church bells are heard in the distance.

PUNTILA: You'll marry the Attaché and that's that. I'm not giving you a penny otherwise. I'm responsible for your future.

EVA: The other day you were saying I shouldn't marry if he's not a man. I should marry the man I love.

PUNTILA: I say a lot of things when I've had a glass too many. And I don't like your quibbling about what I say. And let me catch you with that driver just once more and I'll give you something to remember. There could easily have been strangers around when you came strolling out of that bath hut together. That would have made a fine scandal. *He suddenly looks into the distance and bellows*: What are the horses doing on the clover?

VOICE: Stableman's orders, sir.

PUNTILA: Get them out of there at once! *To Eva*: All I have to do is go away for the afternoon, and the whole estate's in a mess. And why are the horses on the clover, may I ask? Because the stableman's having it off with the gardener's girl. And why has that fourteen-month heifer been mounted so young that her growth is stunted? Because the girl who looks after the fodder is having it off with my trainee. Of course that leaves her no time for seeing that the bull doesn't mount my heifers, she just lets him loose on whatever he wants. Disgusting. And if the gardener's girl – remind me to speak to her – wasn't always lying around with the stableman I wouldn't have a mere couple of hundredweight of tomatoes for sale this year; how can she have a proper feeling for my tomatoes, they've always been a small goldmine, I'm not standing for all this stuff on my estate, it's ruinous I'm telling you, and that applies to you and the chauffeur too, I'm not having the estate ruined, that's where I draw the line.

EVA: I'm not ruining the estate.

PUNTILA: I warn you. I won't stand for scandal. I fix up a six-thousand mark wedding for you and do everything humanly possible to have you marry into the best circles, it's costing me a forest, you realise what a forest is? and then you start cheapening yourself with any Tom, Dick and Harry and even with a driver.

Matti has appeared in the yard below. He listens.

PUNTILA: I didn't give you that posh education in Brussels so you could chuck yourself at the chauffeur but to teach you to keep your distance from the servants, or else they'll get above themselves and be all over you. Ten paces distance and no familiarities, or chaos sets in, that's my inflexible rule. *Exit into the house.*

The four women from Kurgela appear at the gateway into the yard. They consult, take off their headscarves, put on straw wreaths and send a representative forward. Sandra the telephonist enters the yard.

THE TELEPHONIST: Good morning. Can I see Mr Puntila?

MATTI: I don't think he's seeing anyone today. He's not at his best.

THE TELEPHONIST: He'll see his fiancée, I imagine.

MATTI: Are you and him engaged?

THE TELEPHONIST: In my eyes.

PUNTILA'S VOICE: And I won't have you using words like 'love', it's nothing but another way of saying filth and that's something I'm not standing for at Puntila's. The engagement party's all fixed, I've had a pig killed, that can't be undone now, he's not going to trot quietly back to his trough again just to oblige me and go on eating merely because you've changed your mind, and anyway I've made my arrangements and wish to be left in peace on my estate and I'm having your room locked and you can do what you like about it.

Matti has picked up a long-handled broom and started sweeping the yard.

THE TELEPHONIST: I seem to know that gentleman's voice.

MATTI: Not surprising. It's your fiancé's.

THE TELEPHONIST: It is and it isn't. In Kurgela it sounded different.

MATTI: In Kurgela, was it? Was that when he went to get the legal alcohol?

THE TELEPHONIST: Perhaps the reason I don't recognise it is that things were different then and there was a face went with it, friendly-looking; he was sitting in a car and had the rosy dawn on his face.

MATTI: I know that face and I know that rosy dawn. You'd better go home.

Sly-Grog Emma enters the yard. She pretends not to know the telephonist.

SLY-GROG EMMA: Mr Puntila here? I would like to see him right away.

MATTI: I'm afraid he's not here. But here's his fiancée, would she do instead?

THE TELEPHONIST, *acting*: Am I mistaken, or is that Emma Takinainen who purveys sly grog?

SLY-GROG EMMA: What did you say I purvey? Sly grog? Just because I have to have a little alcohol when I massage the policeman's wife's leg? It's my alcohol the stationmaster's wife chooses to make her famous cherry brandy with, that'll show you how legal it is. And what's that about fiancées? Switchboard Sandra from Kurgela claiming to be engaged to my fiancé Mr Puntila, whose residence this is, if I am not mistaken? That's a bit much, you old ragbag!

THE TELEPHONIST, *beaming*: Look what I have here, you primitive distiller. What's that on my middle finger?

SLY-GROG EMMA: A wart. But what's this on mine? It's me's engaged, not you. With alcohol and ring too.

MATTI: Are both you ladies from Kurgela? We seem to have fiancées there like other people have mice.

Into the yard come Lisu the milkmaid and Manda the chemist's assistant.

MILKMAID *and* CHEMIST'S ASSISTANT *simultaneously*: Does Mr Puntila live here?

MATTI: Are you two from Kurgela? If so then he doesn't live here, I should know, I'm his driver. Mr Puntila is a different gentleman with the same name as the one you are no doubt engaged to.

MILKMAID: But I'm Lisu Jakkara, the gentleman really is engaged to me, I can prove it. *Indicating the telephonist*: And she can prove it too, she's engaged to him as well.

SLY-GROG EMMA *and* THE TELEPHONIST *simultaneously*: Yes, we can prove it, we're all of us lawful.

All four laugh a lot.

MATTI: Well, I'm glad you can prove it. To be honest, if there was only one lawful fiancée I wouldn't be all that interested, but I know the voice of the masses when I hear it. I propose a confederation of Mr Puntila's fiancées. And that raises the fascinating question: what are you up to?

THE TELEPHONIST: Shall we tell him? We've had a personal invitation from Mr Puntila to come to the great engagement party.

MATTI: An invitation like that could easily be like the snows of yesteryear. The nobs might well treat you like four wild geese from the marshes who come flying up after the shooting party's gone home.

SLY-GROG EMMA: Oh dear, that doesn't sound like much of a welcome.

MATTI: I'm not saying you're unwelcome. Only that in a sense you're a bit ahead of yourselves. I'll have to wait for the right moment to bring you on, so that you're welcomed and frankly acknowledged for the fiancées you are.

THE CHEMIST'S ASSISTANT: All we had in mind was a bit of a laugh and some slap and tickle at the dance.

MATTI: If we pick a good moment it may be all right. Soon as things get warmed up they'll be game for something imaginative. Then we could wheel on the four fiancées. The parson will be amazed and the judge will be a changed man and a happier one when he sees how amazed the parson is, but order must prevail or Mr Puntila won't know where he is when our confederation of fiancées comes marching into the room with the Tavastland anthem playing and a petticoat for our flag.

All laugh a lot again.

SLY-GROG EMMA: Do you think there'd be a drop of coffee to spare and a bit of a dance after?

MATTI: That is a demand which the confederation might get acknowledged as reasonable in view of the fact that hopes were aroused and expenses incurred, because I take it you came by train.

SLY-GROG EMMA: Second class!

Fina the parlourmaid carries a big pot of butter into the house.

THE MILKMAID: Real butter!

THE CHEMIST'S ASSISTANT: We walked straight up from the station. I don't know your name, but could you get us a glass of milk perhaps?

MATTI: A glass of milk? Not before lunch, it'll spoil your appetite.

THE MILKMAID: You needn't worry about that.

MATTI: It'd help your visit along better if I got your betrothed a glass of something stronger than milk.

THE MILKMAID: His voice did sound a bit dry.

MATTI: Switchboard Sandra, who knows everything and shares out her knowledge, will understand why I don't go and get milk for you but try to think out a way of getting some aquavit to him.

THE MILKMAID: Is it true that there are ninety cows at Puntila's? That's what I heard.

THE TELEPHONIST: Yes, but you didn't hear his voice, Lisu.

MATTI: I think you'd be wise to make do with the smell of food to start with.

The stableman and the cook carry a slaughtered pig into the house.

THE WOMEN *applaud by clapping*: That ought to go round all right! Bake it till it crackles. Don't forget the marjoram!

SLY-GROG EMMA: D'you think I could unhook my skirt at lunch if nobody's looking? It's a bit tight.

THE CHEMIST'S ASSISTANT: Mr Puntila would *like* to look.

THE TELEPHONIST: Not at lunch.

MATTI: You know what kind of lunch it's to be? You'll be sitting cheek by jowl with the judge of the High Court at Viborg. I'll tell him [*he rams the broomhandle into the ground and addresses it*] 'My lord, here are four impecunious ladies all worried that their case may be rejected. They have walked great distances on dusty country roads in order to join their betrothed. For early one morning ten days ago a fine stout gent in a Studebaker entered the village and exchanged rings with them and engaged himself to them and now he seems to be backing out of it. Do your duty, pronounce your judgement, and watch your step. Because if you fail to protect them a day may come when there's no High Court in Viborg any longer.'

THE TELEPHONIST: Bravo!

MATTI: Then the lawyer will drink your health too. What will you tell him, Emma Takinainen?

SLY-GROG EMMA: I shall tell him I'm glad to have this contact and would you be so good as to do my tax return for me and keep the inspectors in line. Use your gift of the gab to reduce my husband's military service, our patch of land is too much for me and the colonel's got a down on him. And see that our storekeeper doesn't cheat me when he puts my sugar and paraffin on the slate.

MATTI: You made good use of that opening. But the tax thing only applies if you don't get Mr Puntila. Whoever gets him can afford to pay tax. Then you'll be drinking with the doctor; what'll you say to him?

THE TELEPHONIST: Doctor, I shall say to him, I've those pains in my back again, but don't look so sad, grit your teeth, I'll be paying your bill soon as I've married Mr Puntila. And take your time over me, we're only on the first course, the water for the coffee's not even on yet, and you're responsible for the people's health.

The labourers roll two beer barrels into the house.

SLY-GROG EMMA: That's beer going in.

MATTI: And then you'll be sitting with the parson too. What'll you say to him?

THE MILKMAID: I shall say from now on I'll have time to go to church Sundays any time I feel in the mood.

MATTI: That's not enough for a lunch-time conversation. So I shall add this: 'Your Reverence, the sight today of Lisu the milkmaid eating off a china plate must give you the greatest pleasure, for in God's sight all are equal, so say the scriptures, so why not in that of Mr Puntila? And as the new lady of the manor she'll be sure that you get a little something, the usual few bottles of wine for your birthday, so you can go on saying fine things from your pulpit about the heavenly pastures, now that she no longer has to go out into the earthly pastures to milk the cows.'

In the course of Matti's big speeches Puntila has come out on to the veranda.

PUNTILA: Let me know when you get to the end of your speech. Who are these people?

THE TELEPHONIST, *laughing*: Your fiancées, Mr Puntila, d'you not know them?

PUNTILA: I don't know any of you.

SLY-GROG EMMA: Of course you know us, look at our rings.

THE CHEMIST'S ASSISTANT: Off the curtain-pole at the chemist's in Kurgela.

PUNTILA: What d'you want here? Kick up a stink?

MATTI: Mr Puntila, it mayn't be the ideal moment, in mid-morning so to speak, but we were just discussing how we could contribute to the engagement celebrations at Puntila Hall and we've founded a Confederation of Mr Puntila's fiancées.

PUNTILA: Why not a trade union while you're about it? Things like that shoot up like mushrooms when you're around the place. I know which paper you read.

SLY-GROG EMMA: It's just for a bit of a laugh and maybe a cup of coffee.

PUNTILA: I know those laughs of yours. You've come round to blackmail me into giving you something, you scroungers.

SLY-GROG EMMA: No, no, no.

PUNTILA: I'll give you something to remember me by all right; thought you'd have a high old time because I acted friendly to you, didn't you? You'd best clear out before I have the lot of you thrown off the estate and telephone the police. You're the telephonist at Kurgela, aren't you? I'll ring your supervisor and see if that's the sort of laughs they allow in the public service, and as for the rest of you I'll find out who you are soon enough.

SLY-GROG EMMA: We get it. You know, Mr Puntila, it was more for old times' sake. I think I'll just sit down in your yard so I can say 'I was sitting at Puntila's once, I was invited'. *She sits on the ground.* There, now nobody can say any different, this is me sitting. I needn't say it was on no chair but the bare soil of Tavastland about which the school books say it's hard work but the work's worth while, though not of course who does the work or whose while it is worth. Did I or didn't I smell a calf roasting, and wasn't there some beer?

She sings:

For the Tavastlander clasps his country to his heart
With its lakes and its trees and the clouds above its hills
From its cool green woods to its humming paper mills.

And now help me, girls, don't leave me sitting in this historic position.

PUNTILA: Get off my land.

The four women throw their straw wreaths on the ground and leave the yard. Matti sweeps the straw into a pile.

8

Tales from Finland

Country road. Evening. The four women are walking home.

SLY-GROG EMMA: How's one to tell what sort of a mood they'll be in? When they've been on the booze they're full of jokes and pinching your you-know-what, and it's all you can do to stop them getting intimate and straight into the old hay; then five minutes later something's hit their liver and all they want is call the police. I think I got a nail in my shoe.

THE TELEPHONIST: The sole's half off.

THE MILKMAID: It wasn't made for five hours' walking on a country road.

SLY-GROG EMMA: I've worn it out. Should have lasted

another year. A stone's what I need. *They all sit down, and she bangs the nail in her shoe flat.* As I was saying, you never know where you are with that lot, sometimes they're one way, sometimes another till your head spins. The last police sergeant's wife used often to send for me to massage her poor swollen feet in the middle of the night, and every time she was different according to how she was getting on with her husband. He was having it off with the maid. Time she gave me a box of chocolates I knew he'd sent the girl packing, but a moment later apparently he'd started seeing her again, 'cause however hard she tried racking her brains she just couldn't remember I'd given her twelve massages that month, not six. All of a sudden her memory had gone.

THE CHEMIST'S ASSISTANT: Other times it works out all right for them. Like Chicago Charlie who made a fortune over there, then came back to his relatives twenty years later. They were so poor they used to beg potato peelings from my mother, and when he arrived they served him roast veal to sweeten him up. As he scoffed it he told them he'd once lent his granny fifty marks and it was disturbing to find them so badly off they couldn't even settle their debts.

THE TELEPHONIST: They know what they're up to all right. Must be some reason why they get so rich. There was this landowner our way got one of the tenants to drive him across the frozen lake in the winter of 1908. They knew there was a break in the ice, but they didn't know where, so the tenant had to walk in front the whole seven miles or so. The boss got frightened and promised him a horse if they got to the other side. When they'd got half-way he spoke again and said, 'If you find the way all right and I don't fall through I'll see you get a calf.' Then they saw the lights of some village and he said, 'Keep it up and you'll have earned that watch.' Fifty yards from the shore he was talking about a sack of potatoes, and when they got there he gave him one mark and said, 'Took your time, didn't you?' We're too stupid for their jokes and tricks and we fall for them every time. Know why? 'Cause they look just the same as our sort, and that's what fools us. If they looked like bears or rattlesnakes people might be more on their guard.

THE CHEMIST'S ASSISTANT: Never lark with them and never accept anything from them.

SLY-GROG EMMA: Never accept anything from them: I like that, when they've got everything and us nothing. Try not accepting anything from the river when you're thirsty.

THE CHEMIST'S ASSISTANT: I've got a thirst like a horse, girls.

THE MILKMAID: Me too. At Kausala there was a girl went with the son of the farm where she worked as a maid. There was a baby, but when it all came to court in Helsinki he denied everything so as not to pay maintenance. Her mother had hired a barrister, and he produced the letters the fellow wrote from the army. They spelled it all out and could have got him five years for perjury. But when the judge read out the first letter, took his time over it, he did, she stepped up and asked for them back, so she got no maintenance. She was crying buckets, they said, when she came out of court carrying the letters, and her mother was livid and he laughed himself silly. That's love for you.

THE TELEPHONIST: It was a stupid thing to do.

SLY-GROG EMMA: But that kind of thing can be clever, it all depends. There was a fellow up near Viborg wouldn't accept anything from them. He was in the 1918 business with the Reds, and at Tammerfors they put him in a camp for that, such a young chap, he was so hungry he had to eat grass, not a thing would they give him to eat. His mother went to visit him and took some grub along. Fifty miles each way it was. She lived in a cottage and the landlord's wife gave her a fish to take and a pound of butter. She went on foot except when a farmcart came along and gave her a lift. She told the farmer: 'I'm off to visit my son Athi who's been put in camp with the Reds at Tammerfors, and the landlord's wife has given me a fish for him in the goodness of her heart and this pound of butter.' When the farmer heard this he made her get down because her son was a Red, but as she passed the women doing their washing in the river she again said 'I'm off to Tammerfors to visit my son who's in the Reds' camp there, and the landlord's wife in the goodness of her heart has given me a fish to take him and this pound of butter.' And when she got to the camp at Tammerfors she repeated her story to the commandant and he let her in though normally it was forbidden. Outside the camp the grass was still growing, but behind the barbed wire there was no green grass left, not a leaf on any of the trees, they'd eaten the lot. It's God's truth, you know. She hadn't seen Athi for two years, what with the civil war and him being in that camp, and he was thin as a rake. 'Here you are, Athi, and look, here's a fish and the butter the landlord's wife gave me for you.' Athi said hullo Mum to her and asked after her rheumatism and some of the neighbours, but he wasn't going to accept the fish and the butter at any price, he just got angry and said, 'Did you softsoap the landlord's wife for that stuff? If so you can bloody well carry it back. I'm not accepting nothing from that lot.' She was forced to pack her presents up again, even though Athi was starving, and she said goodbye and went back on foot as before except when a cart came along and gave her a lift. This time she told the farmhand, 'My boy Athi's in prison camp and he refused a fish and some butter because I'd softsoaped the landlord's wife for them and he's not accepting nothing from that lot.' She said the same thing to everybody she met, so it made an impression all along the way, and that was fifty miles.

THE MILKMAID: There *are* fellows like that Athi of hers.

SLY-GROG EMMA: Not enough.

They get up and walk on in silence.

9

Puntila betroths his daughter to a human being

*Dining-room with little tables and a vast sideboard. Parson,
Judge and Lawyer are standing smoking and having coffee. In
the corner sits Puntila, drinking in silence. Next door there is
dancing to the sound of a gramophone.*

THE PARSON: True faith is seldom to be found. Instead we
find doubt and indifference, enough to make one despair of
our people. I keep trying to din it into them that not one
single blackberry would grow but for Him, but they treat the
fruits of nature as entirely natural and gobble them down as
if it was all meant. Part of their lack of faith comes from the
fact that they never go to church, so I am left preaching to
empty pews; as though they lacked transport . . . why,
every milkmaid's got a bicycle; but it's also because of their
inborn wickedness. What other explanation is there when I
attend a deathbed as I did last week and speak of all that
awaits a man in the other life, and he comes up with 'Do you
think this drought's going to spoil the potatoes?'? When you
hear something like that you have to ask yourself if the whole
thing isn't just a waste of time.

THE JUDGE: I feel for you. It's no picnic trying to bash a little
culture into these bumpkins.

THE LAWYER: We lawyers don't have all that easy a time
either. What's always kept us in business has been the small
peasants, those rock-hard characters who'd sooner go on the
parish than forgo their rights. People still get something out
of a quarrel, but they're hampered by their meanness. Much
as they enjoy insulting each other and stabbing one another
and pulling down each other's fences, soon as they realise

that lawsuits cost money their ardour quickly cools and they'll abandon the most promising case for purely mercenary reasons.

THE JUDGE: We live in a commercial age. Everything gets flattened out and the good old institutions disappear. It's dreadfully hard not to lose confidence in our people but to keep on trying to introduce it to a bit of culture.

THE LAWYER: It's all very well for Puntila, his fields grow of their own accord, but a lawsuit's a terribly sensitive plant and by the time it's fully mature your hair will have gone grey. How often do you feel it's all over, it can't last any longer, there can be no further pleas, it's doomed to die young; then something happens and there's a miraculous recovery. It's when it's in its infancy that a case demands the most careful treatment, that's when the mortality figures peak. Once it's been nursed up to adolescence it knows its way around and can manage on its own. A case that has lasted more than four or five years has every prospect of reaching a ripe old age. But the in-between time! It's a dog's life.

Enter the Attaché and the Parson's Wife.

PARSON'S WIFE: Mr Puntila, you mustn't neglect your guests; the Minister's dancing with Miss Eva at the moment, but he has been asking for you.

Puntila doesn't answer.

THE ATTACHÉ: His Reverence's wife made a deliciously witty riposte to my Minister just now. He asked if she appreciated jazz. I was positively on tenterhooks to know how she would deal with that one. She thought for a moment, then she answered well anyway you can't dance to a church organ so it's all the same to her what instruments you use. The Minister laughed himself silly at her joke. Eh, Puntila, what d'you say to that?

PUNTILA: Nothing, because I don't criticise my guests. *He beckons to the Judge.* Freddie, do you like that face?

THE JUDGE: Which one d'you mean?

PUNTILA: The Attaché's. Let's have a straight answer.

THE JUDGE: Go easy, Puntila, that punch is pretty strong.

THE ATTACHÉ *humming the tune being played next door and tapping the time with his feet*: Gets into the old legs, eh what?

PUNTILA *again beckons to the Judge, who does his best not to notice*: Fredrik! Tell me the truth: how do you like it? It's costing me a forest.

The other gentlemen join in and hum 'Je cherche après Titine'.

THE ATTACHÉ *unconscious of what is coming*: I could never remember poetry even at school, but rhythm is in my blood.

THE LAWYER *since Puntila is violently beckoning*: It's a bit warm in here; what about shifting to the drawing-room? *Tries to draw the Attaché away.*

THE ATTACHÉ: Only the other day I managed to remember a line, 'Yes, we have no bananas'! So I have hopes of my memory.

PUNTILA: Freddie! Take a good look at it and let's have your verdict. Freddie!

THE JUDGE: You know the one about the Jew who left his coat hanging in the café. The pessimist said 'He's bound to get it back.' Whereas the optimist said 'Not a hope in hell of his getting it back.'

The gentlemen laugh.

THE ATTACHÉ: And did he get it back?

The gentlemen laugh.

THE JUDGE: I don't think you've entirely seen the point.

PUNTILA: Freddie!

THE ATTACHÉ: You'll have to explain it to me. Surely you got the answers the wrong way round. It's the optimist who ought to be saying 'He's bound to get it back.'

THE JUDGE: No, the pessimist. You see, the joke is that the coat is an old one, and it's better for him if he loses it.

THE ATTACHÉ: Oh I see, it's an old coat? You forgot to mention that. Hahaha! It's the most capital joke I ever heard.

PUNTILA *gets up lowering*: The hour has struck. A fellow like this is more than flesh and blood can bear. Fredrik, you have been avoiding my solemn question about having a face like that in the family. But I am old enough to make up my mind for myself. A person without a sense of humour isn't human. *With dignity*: Leave my house – yes, it's you I'm talking to – stop looking round as if you thought it might be somebody else.

THE JUDGE: Puntila, you are going too far.

THE ATTACHÉ: Gentlemen, I would ask you to forget this incident. You cannot imagine how delicate is the position of a member of the diplomatic corps. The slightest weakness, morally speaking, can lead to the refusal of one's *agrément*. In Paris once, up in Montmartre, the mother-in-law of the Rumanian First Secretary began hitting her lover with an umbrella and there was an irrevocable scandal.

PUNTILA: A scavenger in tails. A scavenger that gobbles up forests.

THE ATTACHÉ, *carried away*: You see the point: it's not that she has a lover, which is normal, nor that she beats him, which is understandable, but that she does it with an umbrella, which is vulgar. A question of nuance.

THE LAWYER: Puntila, he's right, you know. His honour is very vulnerable. He's in the diplomatic service.

THE JUDGE: That punch is too strong for you, Johannes.

PUNTILA: Fredrik, you don't realise how serious the situation is.

THE PARSON: Mr Puntila is a little over-emotional, Anna, perhaps you should see what's going on in the drawing-room.

PUNTILA: There's no danger of my losing control of myself, missis. The punch is its usual self and the only thing that's too much for me is this gentleman's face which I find repugnant for reasons which you can surely understand.

THE ATTACHÉ: My sense of humour was most flatteringly alluded to by the Princess Bibesco when she remarked to Lady Oxford that I laughed at jokes or *bons mots* before they're made, meaning that I'm very quick-witted.

PUNTILA: My god, Freddie, his sense of humour!

THE ATTACHÉ: So long as no names are mentioned it can all be mended, it's only when names and insults are mentioned in the same breath that things are beyond mending.

PUNTILA, *with heavy sarcasm*: Freddie, what am I to do? I can't remember his name; now he's telling me I'll never be able to get rid of him. O thank God, it's just occurred to me that I read his name on an IOU I had to buy back and that it's Eino Silakka; now will he go, do you think?

THE ATTACHÉ: Gentlemen, a name has now been mentioned. From now on every word will have to be most meticulously weighed.

PUNTILA: What can you do? *Suddenly shouting*: Get out of here at once and don't you ever let me catch another glimpse of you at Puntila Hall! I'm not hitching my daughter to a scavenger in tails!

THE ATTACHÉ, *turning to face him*: Puntila, you have begun to be insulting. To throw me out of your house is to cross that fine boundary beyond which scandal sets in.

PUNTILA: It's too much. My patience is giving out. I was going to let you know privately that your face gets on my nerves and you'd better go, but you force me to make myself clear and say 'You shit, get out!'

THE ATTACHÉ: Puntila, I take that amiss. Good day, gentlemen. *Exit.*

PUNTILA: Don't loiter like that! Let me see you run, I'll teach you to give me pert answers!
He hurries after him. All but the judge and the parson's wife follow.

THE PARSON'S WIFE: There'll be a scandal.
Enter Eva.

EVA: What wrong? What's all that din out in the yard?

THE PARSON'S WIFE, *hurrying to her*: My poor child, something unpleasant has occurred, you must arm yourself with courage.

EVA: What's occurred?

THE JUDGE, *fetching a glass of sherry*: Drink this, Eva. Your
    father got outside a whole bowl of punch, then he suddenly
    took exception to Eino's face and threw him out.
EVA: O dear, this sherry's corked. What did he say to him?
THE PARSON'S WIFE: Don't you feel shaken, Eva?
EVA: Yes, of course.
    The parson comes back.
PARSON: Terrible.
THE PARSON'S WIFE: What's terrible? Did something
    happen?
THE PARSON: A terrible scene in the yard. He threw stones
    at him.
EVA: Did he hit him?
THE PARSON: I don't know. The lawyer quickly got between
    them. And to think that the Minister's in the drawing room
    next door.
EVA: Then I'm pretty sure he'll go, Uncle Fredrik. Thank
    heaven we got the Minister along. It wouldn't have been half
    the scandal otherwise.
THE PARSON'S WIFE: Eva!
    Enter Puntila and Matti, followed by Laina and Fina.
PUNTILA: I have just had a profound insight into the depravity
    of this world. In I went with the best of intentions and told
    them that there'd been a mistake, that I'd all but betrothed
    my only daughter to a scavenger but now I'm quickly
    betrothing her to a human being. It has long been my
    ambition to betroth my daughter to a first-rate human being,
    Matti Altonen, a conscientious chauffeur and a friend of
    mine. So you are to drink a toast to the happy couple. What
    kind of response do you think I got? The Minister, whom
    I'd taken for an educated man, looked at me like something
    the cat had brought in and called for his car. And the others
    naturally followed him like sheep. Sad. I felt like a Christian
    martyr among the lions and gave them a piece of my mind.
    He cleared off quickly but I managed to catch him by his car,
    I'm pleased to say, and told him he's a shit too. I take it I

was voicing the general opinion?

MATTI: Mr Puntila, suppose the two of us went into the kitchen and discussed the whole thing over a bowl of punch?

PUNTILA: Why the kitchen? We've done nothing yet to celebrate your engagement, only the other one. A bit of a mistake. Put the tables together, you people, make me a festive board. We're going to celebrate. Fina, you come and sit by me. *He sits down in the middle of the room while the others bring the little tables together to make one long table in front of him. Eva and Matti together fetch chairs.*

EVA: Don't look at me like my father inspecting a smelly breakfast egg. Not so long ago you were looking at me quite differently.

MATTI: That was for show.

EVA: Last night when you wanted to take me catching crayfish on the island it wasn't to catch crayfish.

MATTI: That was night-time, and it wasn't to get married either.

PUNTILA: Parson, you sit next the maid. Mrs Parson next the cook. Fredrik, come and sit at a decent table for once. *They all sit down reluctantly. Silence ensues.*

THE PARSON'S WIFE, *to Laina*: Have you started bottling your this year's mushrooms yet?

LAINA: I don't bottle them, I dry them.

THE PARSON'S WIFE: How do you do that?

LAINA: I cut them in chunks, string them together with a needle and thread and hang them in the sun.

PUNTILA: I want to say something about my daughter's fiancé. Matti, I've had my eye on you and I've got an idea of your character. To say nothing of the fact that there've been no more mechanical breakdowns since you came to Puntila Hall. I respect you as a human being. I've not forgotten that episode this morning. I saw how you looked as I stood on the balcony like Nero and drove away beloved guests in my blindness and confusion; I told you about those attacks of mine. All through tonight's party, as you may

have noticed – or must have guessed if you weren't there –
I sat quiet and withdrawn, picturing those four women
trudging back to Kurgela on foot after not getting a single
drop of punch, just harsh words. I wouldn't be surprised if
their faith in Puntila were shaken. I ask you, Matti: can you
forget that?

MATTI: Mr Puntila, you can treat it as forgotten. But please use
all your authority to tell your daughter that she cannot marry
a chauffeur.

THE PARSON: Very true.

EVA: Daddy, Matti and I had a little argument while you were
outside. He doesn't think you'll give us a sawmill, and won't
believe I can stand living with him as a simple chauffeur's
wife.

PUNTILA: What d'you say to that, Freddie?

JUDGE: Don't ask me, Johannes, and stop looking at me like
the Stag at Bay. Ask Laina.

PUNTILA: Laina, I put it to you, do you think I'm a man who'd
economise on his daughter and think a sawmill and a flour
mill plus a forest too much for her?

LAINA, *interrupted in the midst of a whispered conversation
with the parson's wife about mushrooms, judging from the
gestures*: Let me make you some coffee, Mr Puntila.

PUNTILA: Matti, can you fuck decently?

MATTI: I'm told so.

PUNTILA: That's nothing. Can you do it indecently? That's
what counts. But I don't expect an answer. I know you never
blow your own trumpet, you don't like that. But have you
fucked Fina? So I can ask her? No? Extraordinary.

MATTI: Can we change the subject, Mr Puntila?

EVA, *having drunk a bit more, gets to her feet and makes a
speech*: Dear Matti, I beseech you make me your wife so I
may have a husband like other girls do, and if you like we
can go straight off to catch crayfish without nets. I don't
consider myself anything special despite what you think, and
I can live with you even if we have to go short.

PUNTILA: Bravo!

EVA: But if you don't want to go after crayfish because you feel it's too frivolous then I'll pack a small case and drive off to your mother's with you. My father won't object . . .

PUNTILA: Quite the contrary, only too delighted.

MATTI *likewise stands up and quickly knocks back two glasses*: Miss Eva, I'll join you in any piece of foolishness you like, but take you to my mother's, no thanks, the old woman would have a stroke. Why, there's hardly so much as a sofa at her place. Your Reverence, describe Miss Eva a pauper kitchen with sleeping facilities.

THE PARSON *solemnly*: Extremely poverty-stricken.

EVA: Why describe it? I shall see for myself.

MATTI: Try asking my old lady where the bathroom is.

EVA: I shall use the public sauna.

MATTI: On Mr Puntila's money? You've got your sights on that sawmill-owner, but he isn't materialising, 'cause Mr Puntila is a sensible person or will be when he comes to first thing in the morning.

PUNTILA: Say no more, say no more about that Puntila who is our common enemy; that's the Puntila who was drowned in a bowl of punch this evening, the wicked fellow. Look at me now, I've become human, all of you drink too, become human, never say die!

MATTI: I'm telling you I just can't take you to my mother's, she'd hammer my ears with her slippers if I brought home a wife like that, if you really want to know.

EVA: Matti, you shouldn't have said that.

PUNTILA: The girl's right, you're going too far, Matti. Eva has her faults and she may finish up a bit on the fat side like her mother, but not before she's thirty or thirty-five, at the moment I could show her anywhere.

MATTI: I'm not talking about fat, I'm saying she's hopelessly unpractical and no kind of wife for a chauffeur.

THE PARSON: I entirely agree.

MATTI: Don't laugh, Miss Eva. You'd laugh on the other side

of your face if my mother tested you out. You'd look pretty silly then.

EVA: Matti, let's try. You're the chauffeur and I'm your wife; tell me what I'm supposed to do.

PUNTILA: That's what I like to hear. Get the sandwiches, Fina, we'll have a snug meal while Matti tests Eva till she's black and blue all over.

MATTI: You stay there, Fina, we've no servants; when unexpected guests turn up we've just got what's generally in the larder. Bring on the herring, Eva.

EVA, *cheerfully*: I won't be a moment. *Exit.*

PUNTILA *calls after her*: Don't forget the butter. *To Matti*: I like the way you're determined to stand on your own feet and not accept anything from me. Not everyone would do that.

THE PARSON'S WIFE *to Laina*: But I don't salt my field mushrooms, I cook them in butter with some lemon, the little button ones I mean. I use blewits for bottling too.

LAINA: I don't count blewits as really delicate mushrooms, but they don't taste too bad. The only delicate ones are field mushrooms and cêpes.

EVA, *returning with a dish of herring*: We've no butter in our kitchen, right?

MATTI: Ah, there he is. I recognise him. *He takes the dish.* I met his brother only yesterday and another relative the day before; in fact I've been meeting members of his family ever since I first reached for a plate. How many times a week would you like to eat herring?

EVA: Three times, Matti, if need be.

LAINA: It'll need be more than that, like it or not.

MATTI: You've a lot to learn still. When my mother was cook on a farm she used to serve it five times a week. Laina serves it eight times. *He takes a herring and holds it up by the tail*: Welcome, herring, thou filler of the poor! Thou morning, noon and night fodder, and salty gripe in the guts! Out of the sea didst thou come, and into the earth shalt thou go. By thy power are forests cut down and fields sown, and by thy power go those machines called farmhands which have not as yet achieved perpetual motion. O herring, thou dog, but for thee we might start asking the farmers for pig meat, and what would come of Finland then?

He puts it back, cuts it up and gives everyone a small piece.

PUNTILA: It tastes to me like a delicacy because I eat it so seldom. That sort of inequality shouldn't be allowed. Left to myself I'd put all the income from the estate in a single fund, and if any of my staff wanted money they could help themselves, because if it weren't for them there'd be nothing there. Right?

MATTI: I wouldn't recommend it. You'd be ruined in a week and the bank would take over.

PUNTILA: That's what you say, but I say different. I'm practically a communist, and if I were a farmhand I'd make old Puntila's life hell for him. Go on with your test, I find it interesting.

MATTI: If I start to think what a woman has to be able to do before I can present her to my mother then I think of my socks. *He takes off a shoe and gives his sock to Eva.* For instance, how about darning that?

THE JUDGE: It is a lot to ask. I said nothing about the herring, but even Juliet's love for Romeo would hardly have weathered such an imposition as darning his socks. Any love that is capable of so much self-sacrifice could easily become uncomfortable, for by definition it is too ardent and therefore liable to make work for the courts.

MATTI: Among the lower orders socks are not mended for love but for reasons of economy.

THE PARSON: I doubt if the pious sisters who taught her in Brussels had quite this sort of thing in mind.

Eva has returned with needle and thread and starts sewing.

MATTI: If she missed out on her education she'll have to make up for it now. *To Eva:* I won't hold your upbringing against you so long as you show willing. You were unlucky in your choice of parents and never learned anything that matters. That herring just now showed what vast gaps there are in your knowledge. I deliberately picked socks because I wanted to see what sort of stuff you're made of.

FINA: I could show Miss Eva how.

PUNTILA: Pull yourself together, Eva, you've a good brain, you're not going to get this wrong.

Eva reluctantly gives Matti the sock. He lifts it up and inspects it with a sour smile, for it is hopelessly botched.

FINA: I couldn't have done it any better without a darning egg.

PUNTILA: Why didn't you use one?

MATTI: Ignorance. *To the judge, who is laughing*: It's no laughing matter, the sock's ruined. *To Eva*: If you're dead set on marrying a chauffeur it's a tragedy because you'll have to cut your coat according to your cloth and you can't imagine how little of that there is. But I'll give you one more chance to do better.

EVA: I admit the sock wasn't brilliant.

MATTI: I'm the driver on an estate, and you help out with the washing and keeping the stoves going in winter. I get home in the evening, how do you receive me?

EVA: I'll be better at that, Matti. Come home.

Matti walks away a few paces and pretends to come in through a door.

EVA: Matti! *She runs up to him and kisses him.*

MATTI: Mistake number one. Intimacies and lovey-dovey when I come home tired.

He goes to an imaginary tap and washes. Then he puts out his hand for a towel.

EVA *has started talking away*: Poor Matti, you tired? I've spent all day thinking how hard you work. I wish I could do it for you. *Fina hands her a towel, which she disconsolately passes to Matti.*

EVA: I'm sorry. I didn't realise what you wanted.

Matti gives a disagreeable growl and sits down at the table. Then he thrusts his boot at her. She tries to tug it off.

PUNTILA *has stood up and is following with interest*: Pull!

THE PARSON: I would call that a remarkably sound lesson. You see how unnatural it is.

MATTI: That's something I don't always do, but today you see I was driving the tractor and I'm half dead, and that has to be allowed for. What did you do today?

EVA: Washing, Matti.

MATTI: How many big items did you have to wash?

EVA: Four. Four sheets.

MATTI: You tell her, Fina.

FINA: You'll have done seventeen at least and two tubs of coloureds.

MATTI: Did you get your water from the hose, or did you have to pour it in by the bucket 'cause the hose wasn't working like it doesn't at Puntila's?

PUNTILA: Give me stick, Matti, I'm no good.

EVA: By the bucket.

MATTI: Your nails [*he takes her hand*] have got broken scrubbing the wash or doing the stove. Really you should always put a bit of grease on them, that's the way my mother's hands got [*he demonstrates*] swollen and red. I'd say you're tired, but you'll have to wash my livery, I'm afraid. I have to have it clean for tomorrow.

EVA: Yes, Matti.

MATTI: That way it'll be properly dry first thing and you won't have to get up to iron it till five-thirty.

Matti gropes for something on the table beside him.

EVA, *alarmed*: What's wrong?

MATTI: Paper.

Eva jumps up and pretends to hand Matti a paper. Instead of taking it he goes on sourly groping around on the table.

FINA: On the table.

Eva finally puts it on the table, but she still has not pulled the second boot off, and he bangs it impatiently. She sits down on the floor once again to deal with it. Once she has got it off he stands up, relieved, snorts and combs his hair.

EVA: I've been embroidering my apron, that'll add a touch of colour, don't you think? You can add touches of colour all over the place if only you know how. Do you like it, Matti? *Matti, disturbed in his reading, lowers the paper exhaustedly and gives Eva a pained look. She is startled into silence.*

FINA: No talking while he's reading the paper.

MATTI, *getting up*: You see?

PUNTILA: I'm disappointed in you, Eva.

MATTI, *almost sympathetically*: Failure all along the line. Wanting to eat herring only three times a week, no egg for darning the sock, then the lack of finer feelings when I arrive home late, not shutting up for instance. And when they call me up at night to fetch the old man from the station; how about that?

EVA: Ha, just let me show you. *She pretends to go to a window and shouts very rapidly*: What, in the middle of the night? When my husband's just got home and needs his sleep? I never heard anything like it. If he's drunk let him sleep it off in a ditch. Sooner than let my husband go out I'll pinch his trousers.

PUNTILA: That's good, you must allow her that.

EVA: Drumming folk up when they should be asleep. As if they didn't get buggered about enough by day. Why, my husband gets home and falls into bed half dead. I'm giving notice. That better?

MATTI, *laughing*: Eva, that's first rate. I'll get the sack of course, but do that act in front of my mother and you'll win her heart. *Playfully he slaps Eva on the bottom.*

EVA, *speechless, then furious*: Stop that at once!

MATTI: What's the matter?

EVA: How dare you hit me there?

THE JUDGE *has stood up, touches Eva on the shoulder*: I'm afraid you failed your test after all, Eva.

PUNTILA: What on earth's wrong with you?

MATTI: Are you offended? I shouldn't have slapped you, that it?

EVA, *able to laugh once more*: Daddy, I doubt if it would work.

THE PARSON: That's the way it is.

PUNTILA: What d'you mean, you doubt?

EVA: And I now see my education was all wrong. I think I'll go upstairs.

PUNTILA: I shall assert myself. Sit down at once, Eva.

EVA: Daddy, I'd better go, I'm sorry, but your engagement party's off, good night. *Exit.*

PUNTILA: Eva!

Parson and judge likewise begin to leave. But the parson's wife is still talking to Laina about mushrooms.

THE PARSON'S WIFE, *with enthusiasm*: You've almost converted me, but bottling them is what I'm used to, I know where I am. But I shall peel them beforehand.

LAINA: You don't have to, you just need to clean off the dirt.

THE PARSON: Come along, Anna, it's getting late.

PUNTILA: Eva! Matti, I'm writing her off. I fix her up with a husband, a marvellous human being, and make her so happy she'll get up every morning singing like a lark; and she's too grand for that, and has doubts. I disown her. *Hurries to the door.* I'm cutting you out of my will! Pack up your rags and get out of my house! Don't think I didn't see you were all set to take the Attaché just because I told you to, you spineless dummy! You're no longer any daughter of mine.

THE PARSON: Mr Puntila, you are not in command of yourself.

PUNTILA: Let me alone, go and preach that stuff in your church, there's nobody to listen there anyway.

THE PARSON: Mr Puntila, I wish you good night.

PUNTILA: Yes, off you go, leaving behind you a father bowed down with sorrow. How the hell did I come to have a daughter like that, fancy catching her sodomising with a scavenging diplomat. Any milkmaid could tell her why the Lord God made her a bottom in the sweat of his brow. That she might lie with a man and slaver for him every time she catches sight of one. *To the judge*: And you too, holding your tongue instead of helping to expel her evil spirit. You'd better get out.

THE JUDGE: That's enough, Puntila, just you leave me be. I'm washing my hands in innocence. *Exit smiling.*

PUNTILA: You've been doing just that for the past thirty years, by now you must have washed them away. Fredrik, you used to have peasant's hands before you became a judge and took to washing them in innocence.

THE PARSON, *trying to disengage his wife from her conversation with Laina*: Anna, it's time we went.

THE PARSON'S WIFE: No, I never soak them in cold water and, you know, I don't cook the stalks. How long do you give them?

LAINA: I bring them to the boil once, that's all.

THE PARSON: I'm waiting, Anna.

THE PARSON'S WIFE: Coming. I let them cook ten minutes.
The parson goes out shrugging his shoulders.

PUNTILA, *at the table once more*: They're not human beings. I can't look on them as human.

MATTI: Come to think of it, they are, though. I knew a doctor once would see a peasant beating his horse and say 'He's treating it like a human being'. 'Like an animal' would have given the wrong impression.

PUNTILA: That is a profound truth, I'd like to have had a drink on that. Have another half glass. I really appreciated your way of testing her, Matti.

MATTI: Sorry to have tickled up your daughter's backside, Mr Puntila, it wasn't part of the test, more meant as a kind of encouragement, but it only showed the gulf between us as you'll have seen.

PUNTILA: Matti, there's nothing to be sorry about. I've no daughter now.

MATTI: Don't be so unforgiving. *To Laina and the parson's wife*: Well, anyway I hope you got the mushroom question settled?

THE PARSON'S WIFE: Then you add your salt right at the start?

LAINA: Right at the start. *Exeunt both.*

PUNTILA: Listen, the hands are still down at the dancing.
From the direction of the lake Red Surkkala is heard singing.

> A countess there lived in the northern countree
> And lovely and fair she was.
> 'Oh forester, see how my garter is loose
> It is loose, it is loose.
> Bend down yourself and tie it for me.'
>
> 'My lady, my lady, don't look at me so.
> I work here because I must eat.
> Your breasts they are white but the axe-edge is cold
> It is cold, it is cold.
> Death is bitter, though loving is sweet.'
>
> The forester fled that very same night.
> He rode till he came to the sea.
> 'Oh boatman, oh take me away in your boat
> In your boat, in your boat.
> Take me away far over the sea.'
>
> A lady fox loved a rooster one day.
> 'Oh handsome, I must be your bride!'
> The evening was pleasant, but then came the dawn
> Came the dawn, came the dawn.
> All of his feathers were spread far and wide.

PUNTILA: That's meant for me. Songs like that cut me to the quick. *Meanwhile Matti has put his arm around Fina and gone dancing off with her.*

10

Nocturne

In the yard. Night. Puntila and Matti making water.

PUNTILA: I could never live in a town. Because I like going straight out and pissing in the open, under the stars, it's the only way I get anything out of it. They say it's primitive in the country, but I call it primitive when you do it into one of those porcelain affairs.

MATTI: I know. You want to keep the sporting element.
Pause.

PUNTILA: I hate it when a fellow can't get any fun out of life. That's what I look for in my men, a sense of fun. When I see someone loafing around with a long face I want to get rid of him.

MATTI: I see your point. I can't think why all those people on the estate look so wretched, all skin and bone and chalky white faces and twenty years older than they should be. I bet they're doing it to tease you, else they'd have the decency not to show themselves around the yard when you got visitors.

PUNTILA: As if anyone went hungry at Puntila's.

MATTI: Even if they did. They ought to be used to hunger in Finland by now. They won't learn, they just aren't prepared to try. 1918 polished off 80,000 of them, and that made it peaceful as paradise. Because there were so many less mouths to feed.

PUNTILA: That sort of thing shouldn't be necessary.

11

Puntila Esquire and his man Matti climb Mount Hatelma

Library at Puntila's. Groaning and with his head wrapped in a wet towel, Puntila is examining accounts. Laina the cook stands beside him with a basin and a second towel.

PUNTILA: If I hear of the Attaché having any more of those half-hour phone calls to Helsinki I shall call the engagement off. I don't so much mind it costing me a forest, but petty thieving makes me throw up. And what are all those blots over the figures in the egg book: am I to keep an eye on the hens too?

FINA, *entering*: His Reverence and the secretary of the milk co-operative would like a word with you.

PUNTILA: I don't want to see them. My head's bursting. I think I'm getting pneumonia. Show them in.
Enter the parson and the lawyer. Fina makes a rapid exit.

THE PARSON: Good morning, Mr Puntila, I trust that you had a restful night. I chanced to run into the secretary and we thought we might drop in to see how you were.

THE LAWYER: A night of misunderstandings, so to speak.

PUNTILA: I spoke to Eino on the telephone, if that's what you mean; he has apologised and that's that.

THE LAWYER: Puntila, my dear fellow, there is a further point which you should perhaps consider. In so far as the misunderstandings that occurred at Puntila Hall concern your family life and your relationship with members of the government they are wholly your own affair. Unfortunately that is not all.

PUNTILA: Don't beat about the bush, Pekka. Any damage

that's been done, I'll pay.

THE PARSON: Unhappily there are some kinds of damage which cannot be repaired by money, my dear Mr Puntila. To put it bluntly, we've come to you in the friendliest spirit to discuss the Surkkala problem.

PUNTILA: What about Surkkala?

THE PARSON: We understood you to say the other day that you wanted to dismiss the man because, as you yourself put it, he was an undesirable influence in the community.

PUNTILA: I said I was going to chuck him out.

THE PARSON: Yesterday was quarter-day, Mr Puntila, but Surkkala cannot have been given notice or I should not have seen his eldest daughter in church.

PUNTILA: What, not given notice? Laina! Surkkala wasn't given notice.

LAINA: No.

PUNTILA: Why not?

EVA: You met him at the hiring fair and brought him back in the Studebaker and instead of giving him notice you gave him a ten-mark note.

PUNTILA: How dare he take ten marks from me when I'd told him more than once he'd have to be out by next quarter-day? Fina! *Enter Fina*. Get me Surkkala right away. *Exit Fina*. I've got this terrible headache.

THE LAWYER: Coffee.

PUNTILA: That's it, Pekka, I must have been drunk. I'm always doing that sort of thing when I've had one too many. I could kick myself. That fellow ought to be in prison, taking an unfair advantage.

THE PARSON: Mr Puntila, that will be it, I am sure. We all know your heart is in the right place. It could only have happened when you were under the influence of drink.

PUNTILA: How appalling. *In despair*: What am I to say to the National Militia? My honour is at stake. Once this gets around I'll be blacklisted. They'll stop buying my milk. It's all Matti's fault, my driver, he sat next to him, I can see the whole thing. He knows I can't bear Surkkala, and allowed me to give him ten marks all the same.

THE PARSON: Mr Puntila, there's no need for you to take this affair too tragically. Such things happen, you know.

PUNTILA: Don't tell me they happen. They'd better stop happening, or I'll get myself made a Ward of Court. I can't drink all my milk myself, I'll be ruined. Pekka, don't just sit there, do something, you're the secretary, I'll make a donation to the National Militia. It's the drink, that's all. Laina, it doesn't agree with me.

THE LAWYER: You'll pay him off then. He must go, he's infecting the atmosphere.

THE PARSON: I think we should leave now, Mr Puntila. No damage is beyond repair so long as one's intentions are good. Good intentions are everything, Mr Puntila.

PUNTILA *shakes his hand*: Thank you very much.

THE PARSON: Nothing to thank us for, we're merely doing our duty. Let's do it quickly.

THE LAWYER: And while you're about it it might be a good idea to find out about the past history of that chauffeur of yours, who makes no very good impression on me either.
Exeunt parson and lawyer.

PUNTILA: Laina, from now on no drop of alcohol shall pass my lips, no, not one. I thought about it this morning when I woke up. It's a curse. I decided to go to the cowshed and make a resolution. I am very fond of my cows. Whatever I resolve in my cowshed stands. *Grandly*: Fetch the bottles out of my stamp cupboard, all of them, and all the alcohol left in the house, I shall destroy it here and now by smashing every single bottle. Never mind how much they cost, Laina, think of the estate.

LAINA: Right, Mr Puntila. But are you absolutely sure?

PUNTILA: That's disgraceful about Surkkala, my not evicting him, it's a frightful lesson to me. Tell Altonen too I want him right away. That fellow's my evil genius.

LAINA: Dear oh dear, they packed everything up once and

now they unpacked it again.

Laina hurries off. Enter Surkkala and his children.

PUNTILA: I said nothing about bringing your brats. You're the one I have to settle with.

SURKKALA: That's what I thought, Mr Puntila, that's why I brought them along, they can listen, it won't do them no harm.

Pause. Enter Matti.

MATTI: Good morning, Mr Puntila, how's the headache?

PUNTILA: Here the bastard comes. What's this I hear about you, up to all kinds of tricks behind my back? Didn't I warn you only yesterday I'd sling you out without a reference?

MATTI: Yes, Mr Puntila.

PUNTILA: Shut up, I'm sick of your insolence and smart answers. My friends have been telling me all about you. How much did Surkkala pay you?

MATTI: I've no idea what you're talking about, Mr Puntila.

PUNTILA: Trying to deny that you and Surkkala are as thick as thieves, are you? You're a Red yourself, managed to stop me getting rid of him just in time, didn't you?

MATTI: Excuse me, Mr Puntila, I was simply carrying out your orders.

PUNTILA: You must have realised those orders were without rhyme or reason.

MATTI: Excuse me, but orders aren't as easily distinguished as you might like. If I stuck to obeying the ones that made sense you'd sack me for idling.

PUNTILA: Don't put words in my mouth, you crook, you know perfectly well I won't stand for elements like that on my farm, agitating till my men refuse to go out on the heathland without an egg for their breakfast, you bolshevik. In my case it's mere alcoholic fuddle stops me giving him notice by the right date so that I have to pay three months' wages to be rid of him; but with you it's planned.

Laina and Fina keep bringing in bottles.

PUNTILA: This time it's serious, Laina. You can see it isn't just a promise but I really am destroying all the alcohol. I never went as far as that on previous occasions, I'm afraid, so I always had alcohol at hand when the weakness came over me. That was the root of all evil. I once read that the first step to temperance was not to buy alcohol. Too few people are aware of that. Once it's there, though, it must at least be destroyed. *To Matti*: As for you, I've a purpose in letting you watch, there's nothing could give you such a fright.

MATTI: That's right, Mr Puntila. Shall I take the bottles out into the yard and smash them for you?

PUNTILA: No, I'll do it myself, you swindler, just the job that'd be for you, eh, destroying this lovely liquor [*he holds up a bottle to inspect it*] by drinking the lot.

LAINA: Don't spend too long looking at that bottle, Mr Puntila, chuck it out of the window.

PUNTILA: Perfectly right. *To Matti, coldly*: You'll never get me to drink liquor again, you filthy fellow. All you care about is to have folk wallowing round you like pigs. True love of your work is something you just don't know, you'd never stir a finger if you didn't have to keep yourself from starving, you parasite. Making up to me, eh? Spending night after night telling me dirty stories, then leading me to insult my guests 'cause all you care about is seeing everything dragged into the mire you came from. You're a case for the police, you told me yourself why you were always getting dismissed, and didn't I catch you agitating among those females from Kurgela, a rabble rouser, that's you. *He starts absent-mindedly pouring from the bottle into a glass which his servant Matti has just thoughtfully brought him*. Your attitude to me is one of hatred, and you hope I'll fall for your 'That's right, Mr Puntila' every time.

LAINA: Mr Puntila!

PUNTILA: Don't bother me, there's nothing for you to worry about. I'm only checking up to see if the shop swindled me and to commemorate my inflexible resolve. *To Matti*: But I saw through you from the start and was only watching for you to give yourself away, that's why I got drunk with you but you didn't notice. *He continues to drink.* You thought you could lure me into a life of excess and make whoopee with me just sitting alongside you and boozing, but that's where you made a mistake, my friends have put the finger on you for me and very grateful to them I am, I drink this glass to their healths. I'm appalled when I look back at that life we led, those three days in the Park Hotel, then the trip to find legalised alcohol and those dames from Kurgela, what a life without rhyme or reason, when I think of that milkmaid at dawn trying to take advantage of the fact that I'd had a couple and she'd got big knockers, Lisu I believe she's called. You were always along of course, you rogue, all the same you must admit those were good times, but I'm not giving you my daughter, you swine, but you aren't a shit, I'll say that for you.

LAINA: Mr Puntila, you're drinking again!

PUNTILA: Me drinking? Is that what you call drinking? A bottle or two? *He reaches for the second bottle.* Destroy it [*he hands her the empty one*] smash it, I never want to see it again, you heard what I said. And don't look at me like Our Lord looking at Peter, I can't abide people who split hairs. *Indicating Matti*: That fellow keeps dragging me down, but you lot want me to rot away here till I'm so bored I start biting my toenails. What sort of a life am I leading here? Nothing but having to nag people and tot up the cattle feed day after day. Get out, you pygmies!

Laina and Fina leave, shaking their heads.

PUNTILA, *gazing after them*: Petty. No imagination. *To Surkkala's children*: Rob, steal, become Reds, but don't grow up to be pygmies, that's Puntila's advice to you. *To Surkkala*: Sorry if I'm meddling in your children's education. *To Matti*: Open that bottle.

MATTI: I hope the punch is all right and not peppery like the other day. Uskala needs careful handling, Mr Puntila.

PUNTILA: I know, and careful is my middle name. I always

make my first sip a very small one, so I can spit it out if anything's wrong, if it weren't for being so careful I'd drink the most unspeakable crap. For goodness' sake take a bottle, Matti, I propose to commemorate the resolutions I've made, because they are inflexible, which is a calamity all the same. Here's to you, Surkkala.

MATTI: Does that mean they can stay, Mr Puntila?

PUNTILA: Need we discuss that now, when there's no one else around? Staying is no use to Surkkala, Puntila Hall is too small for him, he doesn't like it here and who can blame him? In his shoes I'd feel exactly the same. I'd look on Puntila as nothing but a capitalist, and you know what I'd do to him? Shove him down a salt mine, that's what I'd like to do, show him what work really is, the old fraud. Am I right, Surkkala? No need to be polite.

SURKKALA'S ELDEST GIRL: But we want to stay, Mr Puntila.

PUNTILA: No, no, Surkkala's going and wild horses couldn't stop him. *He goes to his desk, unlocks it, takes money from the cashbox and hands it to Surkkala.* Less ten. *To the children*: Always be glad you have a father like that, who'll go to the limit for his convictions. You're his eldest, Hella, you must be a support to him. And now it's time to say farewell.

He offers his hand to Surkkala. Surkkala does not take it.

SURKKALA: Come along, Hella, we'll get packed. Now you children have heard all there is to hear at Puntila's, let's go. *Exit with his children.*

PUNTILA, *painfully moved*: My hand's not good enough for him. Didn't you see me waiting for him to make a gesture as we said goodbye, for some kind of word on his side? It never came. The farm means nothing to him. Rootless. Doesn't know the meaning of home. That's why I let him go, like he insisted. A painful episode. *He drinks.* You and me, Matti, we're not that sort. You are a friend and support on my arduous path. Just looking at you gives me a thirst. How much do I pay you?

MATTI: Three hundred a month, Mr Puntila.

PUNTILA: I'm putting you up to three hundred and fifty. Because I'm particularly pleased with you. *Dreamily*: Matti, one of these days I'd like to take you to climb Mount Hatelma, where there's that famous view, so I can show you what a splendid country you live in, you'll kick yourself for not realising it earlier. Shall we climb Mount Hatelma, Matti? It's not all that impossible, I'd say. We could do it in spirit. Given a chair or two we could.

MATTI: I'll do whatever you fancy, any day of the week.

PUNTILA: I wonder if you have the imagination?

Matti is silent.

PUNTILA *bursts out*: Make me a mountain, Matti! Spare no effort, leave no stone unturned, take the biggest rocks or it'll never be Mount Hatelma and we shan't have any view.

MATTI: Everything shall be done as you wish, Mr Puntila. And I realise an eight-hour day's out of the question if you want a mountain in the middle of the valley.

Matti kicks a valuable grandfather clock and a massive gun locker to pieces, using the wreckage together with a number of chairs to build Mount Hatelma in a fury on top of the big billiard table.

PUNTILA: Take that chair there! You won't get a proper Mount Hatelma unless you follow my directions, because I know what's necessary and what isn't and I have the responsibility. You might easily make a mountain that doesn't pay, in other words provides no view for me and gives me no pleasure, because you see all you're interested in is having enough work, it's I who have to give it a useful objective. And now I need a path up the mountain, and one that allows me to drag my sixteen stone up in comfort. Without a path I'd say stuff your mountain, so you see you don't really think. I know how to motivate people, I wonder how you would motivate yourself.

MATTI: There you are, mountain's ready, you can climb up it now. It's a mountain complete with path, not one of those half-finished ones like God created in such a hurry 'cause he only had six days so that he had to go on and create a whole horde of servants for you to tackle things with, Mr Puntila.

PUNTILA *starts to climb up it*: I shall break my neck.

MATTI, *gripping him*: That's something you can do on level ground if I don't prop you.

PUNTILA: It's why I'm taking you, Matti. Else you'd never see the lovely country which bore you and without which you'd be crap, so be grateful to it.

MATTI: I'm grateful to it unto death, but I'm not sure that's enough, because the 'Helsinki Sanomat' says you have to be grateful beyond death too.

PUNTILA: First come fields and meadows, then the forest. With its fir trees that can survive among rocks and live on nothing, you'd be amazed how little they need to get by.

MATTI: The ideal servants, so to speak.

PUNTILA: We're climbing, Matti; Excelsior! Leaving behind us buildings and structures put up by human hands we enter the pure realm of nature, which adopts a more austere countenance. Shake off all your petty cares and abandon yourself to the mighty sensation, Matti!

MATTI: I'm doing the best I can, Mr Puntila.

PUNTILA: Oh thou blessed Tavastland! One more pull at the bottle, that we may see the full extent of thy beauty!

MATTI: Half a mo while I dash back down the mountain and fetch up the plonk.

He climbs down, then up again.

PUNTILA: I wonder if you can see the whole beauty of this country. Are you a Tavastlander?

MATTI: Yes.

PUNTILA: Then let me ask you: where else is there a sky like the sky above the Tavast country? They say there are places where it is bluer, but the moving clouds are more delicate here, the Finnish winds are kindlier, and I wouldn't want a different blue even if I could have it. And when the wild swans take off with that rushing sound from the marshy lakes, is that nothing? Don't you listen to what they say about other places, Matti, they're having you on, just stick to Tavastland, that's my advice.

MATTI: Yes, Mr Puntila.

PUNTILA: The lakes, for instance! Never mind the forests, so far as I am concerned, mine are over that way, I'm having the one on the point cut down; just take the lakes, Matti, just take one or two of them, forget the fish they're so full of, just take the way the lakes look in the morning and it's enough to stop you ever wanting to leave or you'd waste away in foreign parts and die of homesickness; and we've got eight thousand of them in Finland.

MATTI: Right, I'll just take the way they look.

PUNTILA: See that little tug with a bow like a bulldog, and the tree trunks in the morning light? The way they swim along in the tepid water, beautifully bundled and stripped, a small fortune. I can smell fresh timber ten miles off, can you? And talking of the smells we have in the Tavast country, that's a chapter on its own, the berries for instance. After it has rained. And the birch trees, when you come out of the sauna and get whipped with a stout bush, and even in bed next morning, how they smell! Where else do you find that? Where on earth is there such a view?

MATTI: Nowhere, Mr Puntila.

PUNTILA: I like it best when it goes all hazy, like those instants in love when you close your eyes and there's a haze round everything. Though I don't think you get that kind of love outside Tavastland either.

MATTI: Where I was born we used to have caves with rocks outside them round as cannon balls polished all over.

PUNTILA: I bet you used to creep inside? Instead of minding the cows? Hey, I can see some. They're swimming across the lake.

MATTI: I see them. Must be at least fifty head.

PUNTILA: At least sixty. There goes the train. If I listen carefully I can hear the milk churns rattling.

MATTI: If you listen really carefully.

PUNTILA: And I haven't shown you Tavasthus yet, the old place, we've got cities too, I can pick out the Park Hotel, they keep a decent wine there, I can recommend it. We'll pass over the castle, they've turned it into a women's prison for politicals, what business have they got meddling in politics anyway, but the steam mills make a nice picture at this range, they brighten up the landscape. And now what do you see to the left?

MATTI: Well, what do I see?

PUNTILA: Eh, fields! You see fields as far as the eye can reach, Puntila's are among them, particularly the heath, the soil's so rich there I can milk the cows three times a day once I've let them into the clover, and the wheat grows up to your chin and twice a year at that. Join in now!

> And the waves on the beautiful Roina
> Are kissing the milky-white sand.

Enter Fina and Laina.

FINA: Lawks!

LAINA: They've smashed up the whole library.

MATTI: We're just standing on top of Mount Hatelma enjoying the panorama.

PUNTILA: Join in! Where's your feeling for your country?

ALL *except Matti*:

> And the waves on the beautiful Roina
> Are kissing the milky-white sand.

PUNTILA: O Tavastland, blessed art thou! With thy sky, thy lakes, thy people and thy forests! *To Matti*: Tell me that your heart swells at the sight of it all.

MATTI: My heart swells at the sight of your forests, Mr Puntila.

12

Matti turns his back on Puntila

The yard at Puntila's. It is early morning. Matti comes out of the house with a suitcase. Laina follows with a packed lunch.

LAINA: Here, take your lunch, Matti. I can't think why you're going. Why not wait anyway till Mr Puntila's up?

MATTI: I'd sooner not risk having him wake. He was that pissed last night he was promising me in the early hours to make over half his forest to me, and in front of witnesses too. When he hears that he'll send for the police.

LAINA: But if you leave without a reference you'll be ruined.

MATTI: What's the good of a reference if he's either going to write that I'm a Red or that I'm a human being? Neither will get me a job.

LAINA: He won't be able to manage without you now he's so used to you.

MATTI: He'll have to soldier on alone. I've had enough. I can't take his familiarities after that business with Surkkala. Thanks for the lunch and goodbye, Laina.

LAINA, *sniffing*: Have a good trip. *Goes in quickly.*

MATTI, *after walking a few paces*:

> The hour for taking leave has struck
> So, Puntila, I wish you luck.
> I've met them worse than you and twice as tough
> You're half-way human when you've drunk enough.
> But matiness dissolves in boozer's gloom
> It's back to normal and the old 'Who whom?'
> And if it's sad to find out in the end

That oil and water cannot ever blend
Let's waste no tears, there's nothing we can do:
It's time your servants turned their backs on you.
They'll find they have a master really cares
Once they're the masters of their own affairs.

He walks rapidly away.

The Puntila Song

1

Old Puntila went on a three-day blind
In a Tavasthus hotel.
He left an enormous tip behind
But the waiter said 'Go to hell!'
Oh, waiter, how can you insult him so
When life's so gay and sweet?
The waiter replied, 'How am I to know?
I've been far too long on my feet.'

2

The landowner's daughter, Eva P.
A novel once did read.
She marked the place where it told her she
Belonged to a higher breed.
She turned to the chauffeur all the same
And gave his clothes a stare:
'Come sport with me, Mr What's-his-name
I'm told there's a man in there.'

3

Old Puntila met an early bird
As he strolled in the morning dew:
'O milkmaid with the milk-white breasts
Where are you going to?
You're going off to milk my cows
Before cockcrow, I see.
But the best thing for you now you've been roused
Is to come back to bed with me.'

4

The bath hut on the Puntila farm
Is the place for a bit of fun
Where a servant may go to take a bath
While the mistress is having one.
Old Puntila said, 'I'm giving my child
To be a diplomatist's wife.
He won't mind her being a bit defiled
If I'll settle his debts for life.'

5

The landowner's daughter wandered in
To the kitchen at half-past nine:
'O chauffeur, I find you so masculine
Come bring your fishing line.'
'Yes, miss,' the chauffeur replies to her,
'I can see you are ripe for bed.
But can't you see that I prefer
To read my paper instead?'

6

The league of Puntila's would-be brides
Arrived for the nuptial feast.
Old Puntila swore he would have their hides
And roared like a wounded beast.
But when did a sheep get a woollen shirt
Since shearing first began?
'I'll sleep with you, yes, but you're only dirt
In the house of a gentleman.'

7

The women from Kurgela jeered, it is said
When they saw how they'd been foiled
But their shoes and stockings were torn to a shred
And their Sunday was totally spoiled.
And any woman who still believes
That a rich man will honour her claim
Will be lucky to lose no more than her shoes
But she's only herself to blame.

8
Old Puntila thumped on the table, piled
With glorious wedding cake:
'How could I ever betroth my child
To this slab of frozen hake?'
He wanted his servant to have her instead
But the servant first wanted to try her
And finally said, 'I'm not having her.
She has none of what I require.'

Notes on the music

The Ballad of the Forester and the Countess *was written to the tune
of an old Scottish ballad, the* Plum Song *to a folk tune.*

The Puntila Song *has been composed by Paul Dessau. During scene
changes the actress playing Laina the cook comes before the curtain
with a guitarist and an accordion player, and sings the verse
corresponding to the scene just performed. Meanwhile she does various
jobs in preparation for the great engagement party, such as sweeping
the floor, dusting, kneading dough, beating egg whites, greasing cake
tins, polishing glasses, grinding coffee and drying plates.*

Editorial note

Brecht's song provides no verses for scenes 4, 10, 11 nor (more
understandably) 12. In case these scenes are played, the following
verses in similar style and metre might serve the same function.

3a
He drove to the fair to hire some men
And quell his raging thirst
But he thought it a terrible insult when
A neighbour approached them first.
Old Puntila gave them his word and his hand

Till his servant said, 'All very fine
But they won't come unless they know where they stand.
You must sign on the dotted line.'

9
The stars in the Finnish summer night
Are a vision not to miss
And Puntila felt they were never so bright
As when he was having a piss.
'I detest black looks,' he said to his mate.
'They stab me like a knife.
'Why can't my men appreciate
'The joys of an outdoor life?'

10
Old Puntila stood on a lofty peak
To view the country round
And said, 'This landscape is unique
The economy too is sound.
We need to exploit our resources, my friend
And a thousand flowers will bloom.'
But his servant replied, 'Won't a lot depend
On who is exploiting whom?'

Notes and Variants

A Finnish Bacchus
by Hella Wuolijoki

'Enough of that,' said Madam Maria, laying her well-manicured white fingers on the table in a conclusive gesture. 'I insist that Farmer Punttila gets invited to my birthday. I am not having my daughter-in-law's father left out of the party.'

Toini sank her elegant teeth into her cake and passed the butter to her husband's father. He was a pillar of society: Consul, factory owner, engineer, and much more. 'All right. Then on your head be it, Mother. Nothing ever gets celebrated here without brandy, and Father will make such a fool of himself in front of your English guests that we shall never hear the last of it.'

The Consul said something inaudible behind his newspaper.

'Mother's just not thinking of the ghastly consequences there are bound to be,' said Maria's son, chief aide to his father and like him an engineer. 'But after all it's her birthday, and if Mother has set her mind on it there's nothing to be done.'

Maria smiled as she watched her sister-in-law distractedly shovelling sugar into her coffee. 'Leave a little space for the coffee, Hanna dear.' Miss Hanna pushed her cup aside. 'It's all very well for you to laugh, Maria, but you've never had to look after Farmer Punttila like I have.'

'Well, well,' said the master of the house, putting down his paper. 'That's not the worst of our worries. Fina, can you go and get me some hot coffee?'

Fina, the old parlourmaid in her neat white apron, gave a curtsey and disappeared.

'We must have something better for our foreign guests, either a proper butler or at least smarter servants than that rustic parlourmaid of yours.'

Madam Maria's coffee cup halted in mid-air, and this time her smile had more edge to it. 'You're quite wrong, Markus, if you think I'm going to turn our house upside down for your foreign guests, let alone make an Englishman's country seat out of it. Old Fina and my peasant girls will do their jobs properly and your guests can lump it. That's second nature to any well-brought-up visitor.'

'You win,' said the Consul, as he left the table. The engineer pushed his chair back. 'Mother, you really are impossible.' His wife folded up her napkin and put it in its sachet. 'Mother knows her own mind.' Maria and Aunt Hanna were left on their own.

'I like old Punttila,' said Madam Maria, 'better than I like his daughter. You shouldn't get so worked up, Hanna.'

Aunt Hanna peered venomously into her coffee cup. 'You ought to realise that Markus's position creates certain social obligations. And it is up to us to see that these foreign visitors get the right impression of our country.'

Maria gave a clear, disrespectful laugh, and Aunt Hanna went off in dudgeon.

＊   ＊   ＊

The evening before the birthday the main building of the home farm was lit up for the occasion, even though the lady of the house had gone to sleep following the usual eve-of-birthday serenade to which she had been treated. In the servants' hall sat the hosts' and guests' chauffeurs playing cards, while old Fina took them coffee. In the smoking-room the gentlemen sat over their brandies. They were noisy and at ease. The women were already asleep. Only Aunt Hanna went rustling round the house in her black satin, restless and ready to pounce. From the smoking room Punttila's voice could be heard topping the rest. While waiting for the serenade they had absorbed a few shots of brandy with their coffee, after which came further drinking.

The company was divided strictly according to language. On the sofa sat the English and Finnish bankers with their host, talking in English about the timber business and cursing the Russians for their dumping. By the porcelain stove, however, the prohibition laws were being treated with scant respect, the dominant figure being farmer Punttila, red as a brick, his hair ruffled, and around him the judge, the architect and the engineer. Every now and again Punttila went over to the foreign-language group and clinked glasses.

'So help me God,' said Mr Punttila, 'did I never tell you what happened to that landowner from Joensuu in Tavasthus when he celebrated his name day with Judge Tengbom? He left his coachman waiting for him outside the Park Hotel. The man was served his food and drink out there and slept with the hood over him. A week later they moved on to the City Hotel, where the landowner finally went to bed. Next morning his wife came to collect him. Didn't she look angry and hideous, and did she let him have it, hell! She sat down by his bedside with her tongue going like a millrace for hours on end. The old boy lay under the bedclothes quiet as a mouse, and when he finally got a chance to open his mouth he just whispered: "I say, Maria, fetch my cap from the Park Hotel and all your sins will be forgiven." You know old Tengbom, judge, don't you? A very good health to you Englishmen! My God, d'you know what Tengbom did then? Phew, what pretty girls that man had! What about giving the girls a bit of a song? At the tops of our voices now! Life's not all that bad under prohibition, is it? Do you Englishmen really know how to drink? Cheers to you, then!' A fresh bottle made its appearance on the table. Punttila and the judge struck up a resounding song.

Suddenly the smoking-room door sprang open, and there stood Aunt Hanna, a living reminder of life's blacker aspects. 'Come here, my girl, and sit on my lap,' called Punttila, stretching out a hand towards her. 'I suggest Johannes moderates his voice a bit,' said Miss Hanna, whereupon a marked silence descended. The banking gentlemen got politely to their feet, looked at their watches and were amazed at the lateness of the hour. And although Miss Hanna was offered a chair and sat down, one guest after another took his leave and the host went with them. Finally all that was left in the smoking-room was Punttila's group of drinkers. Then the brandy ran out.

'Bloody temperance home,' exclaimed the outraged Punttila. 'Markus's guests get treated no better than sawdust in this place. Have a heart, Hanna, and get us something to drink! We feel an exceptional urge to sing.'

'It is high time Johannes went to bed like the others, and he knows perfectly well that in this house all the alcohol is in my charge. The booze-up is over.'

Punttila thumped the table with his fist, but the rest of them drifted away. Aunt Hanna visited the card-playing chauffeurs with the same blistering success. Finally the whole house was quiet. The lights were put out, and the perpetual summer twilight revealed the solitary figure of farmer Punttila hunched over the empty glasses and bottles in the smoking-room.

'Bloody house, where they hang up the visitors' guts to dry like underwear!' Punttila's drunkenness was boosting his fiendish energy. He started feeling his way stumblingly through the darkened rooms till he found the door of Aunt Hanna's bedroom. Grabbing a chair he treated Aunt Hanna to a veritable serenade.

'Listen to me, you old squirrel, you old viper, don't you realise that farmer Punttila can get some aquavit into this temperance hotel if he wants to? Damme, Hanna, I'll show you how I can get liquor, and legal liquor at that!'

Punttila slammed the big front door behind him.

'Where is Punttila's chauffeur?'

But the yard was deserted. Dark and empty, the windows of the main house and its neighbouring buildings gazed down at the raging farmer. Nobody answered.

'Damn that for a lark, Punttila can find his own wagon.'

The doors of the garage where the guests' cars were slumbering were bolted. Punttila inspected the lock. 'Call that a lock? . . . God's sakes, I'll smash the whole place in!' A few resounding blows and the doors gaped open. Right at the front stood Punttila's Buick.

Firm foot on the accelerator, that's what it takes. A mudguard hits the door. Out, damned mudguard! What does one wretched mudguard cost? Johannes Punttila can get new ones any time he wants. Let's go!

The car followed a zigzag course from side to side of the road. 'I'll straighten out those curves, just watch me!'

In this way farmer Punttila pursued his narrow road to Heaven and rejoiced over each telegraph pole he managed to miss. 'Get out of my way!' he yelled at the telegraph pole at the entrance to the village, and lo! the pole evaded the car of so powerful a farmer.

The village was a fair size. How could one get hold of a prescription for alcohol?

But Punttila knew his way around. He stopped his car at the first hut he came to and started banging on the door as hard as he could.

'Haven't you a cow doctor in this village?' he yelled.

A sleepy old woman opened her window. 'What do you mean going round breaking down decent people's front doors, you drunken lout?'

'I'm just looking for the vet, my little dove,' said Punttila. 'I am farmer Punttila from Lammi, and all my thirty cows have scarlet fever.

So I need legal alcohol.'

'You sodden disgrace! You ought to be ashamed of yourself!'

'Hush, hush, my sweetheart, none of those nasty remarks or I shall smash up your dirty little hovel.'

After which farmer Punttila drove from end to end of the village promising to smash up their hovels, until he found the vet's house. There he leant on the horn of his Buick until the vet's grumpy and loud-mouthed wife opened an upper window. 'Go away! What do you mean by going round drunk, waking people up?'

'Please don't be cross, my darling. I am farmer Punttila from Tavastland, and back home my thirty cows have all got scarlet fever. I need legal alcohol.'

'My husband's asleep. Be off with you!'

'Is that the doctor's wife in person I'm addressing? I wish you a very good day. Kotkotkot, how pretty you are. Please tell the doctor right away that, back in his village, whenever farmer Punttila requires legal alcohol every vet in the place instantly prescribes him the correct dosage.'

The window slammed with a bang.

A renewed barrage on the door.

'Get out, man, I tell you!' and the angry face of the vet appeared at the window above.

'Why, there's the doctor himself. I am farmer Punttila from Tavastland, and my thirty cows have got scarlet fever. What's more I am the biggest bruiser in the whole of Tavastland, and when I want legal alcohol I get some.'

The vet understood his customer exactly and laughed. 'Ah well, if you are such a powerful gentleman then you'll have to have your prescription, I suppose.'

Punttila was most gratified. 'That's it. You are a true vet, ha ha. Come over to us some time and we'll celebrate in style.'

Punttila's car now headed for the chemist's. With one hand Punttila tended the steering wheel, with the other he brandished his prescription for legal alcohol.

The car halted outside the chemist's door. Then Punttila rattled the door violently till two furious women's faces appeared at the upstairs window.

'A very good morning to you. I am farmer Punttila from Tavastland and I've got thirty cows with scarlet fever and I urgently need alcohol.'

The chemist's assistant called down. 'You'd better clear off, an old soak like you disturbing folks' sleep.'

'The summer night was warm/As quiet slept the farm,' sang Punttila. 'Come down and open the door, my little turtledoves! Punttila wishes alcohol. Punttila is well aware that every second house in your village shelters an illegal still. But Punttila insists on having legal alcohol for his beloved cows. If I said my thirty cows had got glanders that, my darlings, would be a vulgar lie, but when I say that Johannes Punttila's cows are down with scarlet fever then it's as good as proven.'

The farmer went on arguing with the chemist's assistant till she opened up and got his alcohol. Back drove Punttila in the direction of the Consular estate.

Glug, glug, glug, went the schnapps bottle in his pocket, and Punttila's drunkenness was on the increase. The telegraph poles got more and more insolent and the road grew narrower and narrower.

'What a problem it is to get through,' sighed Punttila.

But he reached the estate with his honour unimpaired. Glug, glug, glug sang the congenial bottle as farmer Punttila reached Aunt Hanna's door, bottle held high.

'Do you know what I'm carrying in my belly, you miserable old maid? Legal alcohol, glug, glug, d'you hear the lovely music? Fancy thinking Johannes Punttila wasn't going to get his legal alcohol! Now we've something to lace our coffee with!'

The smoking-room was empty and the coffee cold. Punttila took a coffee with schnapps, but in the absence of company it didn't taste as it should. So Punttila went off to find some.

With some difficulty he located the judge's room. 'Hey, judge, look what I've brought you. Come on, just look,' said Punttila, and the judge looked blearily from his bed.

'You've got a bottle, so you have. And now good night.'

'I'm telling you it's a schnapps bottle, judge! Look at the official label, that means legal alcohol.'

The judge turned his face to the wall. 'The court will take a recess,' he murmured and promptly went back to sleep.

Punttila stood there wrapped in thought, observing the judge so prettily asleep between the white bedclothes.

'Too bad you aren't a woman,' sighed Punttila as he felt his way once more through the house. This time he and his bottle managed to locate the kitchen, from which sounds of early morning activity could already be heard.

*   *   *

The mistress of the house was accustomed to waking very early. Today she was fifty. She saw that it was a fine summer morning, thought a little about her life to date, and decided that thinking about it wasn't worth the trouble. She started listening to the sounds of the house. The silence had something menacing about it. She recalled the serenade and the company the previous evening, with Punttila's throaty and compellingly joyous voice following its own erratic path high above all the rest. She was aware of sinister premonitions and could feel the gnawings of conscience.

Madam Maria dressed rapidly and went downstairs. Familiar voices could be heard from the farm kitchen. There sat farmer Punttila with his fortified coffee. Across the table from him three beady-eyed ladies were sitting in judgement on him with severe expressions: Punttila's own two daughters with their golden hair and milk-white complexions, and grumpy Aunt Hanna. The three had gone through the entire litany of all Punttila's sins, from the first bottle to the last, but quite without success. Punttila sat there, his powerful body still buoyed up by the booze, with beaming face and rampant hair. Those fearsome females had caught him in that room, where he had been flirting with the cook and kissing the maid; for he had even been courting old Fina. 'Anyway, Fina, you're better than nothing.'

Punttila had told the story of his nocturnal adventures at least ten times over: how he had driven off to look for legal alcohol and threatened to smash the hovels in. He was overjoyed to see Madam Maria, and started telling it all over again. He was delighted to find that he made her laugh. Then some of the chauffeurs came into the kitchen, so the farmer had to repeat it all once more. The women took the opportunity to move into the dining-room for a council of war.

Maria's daughter-in-law Toini started sobbing: 'What are we to do with him?' 'Chuck him in the lake and drown him where it's deepest,' suggested Aunt Hanna. 'Then Auntie will have to winkle him out of the kitchen before she drowns him,' sighed the other daughter. The mistress of the house laughed: 'If only we could confine him to the kitchen.'

'You asked for it, Maria. Mind out for your dining-room when the guests come down to breakfast. How do you think it's going to look?' hissed Aunt Hanna.

Madam Maria looked out of the window: 'Keep your hair on, children. Let him be his own self, even if it's only when he's drunk.'

Aunt Hanna raised her hands to heaven. 'I wish you joy of whatever happens. Come along, girls.'

Meanwhile farmer Punttila was sitting in the kitchen, an arm round each of the two chauffeurs. 'Shut the door so those women don't disturb us again. Drink up, my boys, farmer Punttila has got legal alcohol. Punttila doesn't give a damn whether you're communists or socialists, so long as you do your job like clockwork. Yes, boys, chopping down the forests and ploughing the fields and digging out stones! That's proper work for a human being. In Punttila's young days there wasn't a bull that he hadn't wrestled on to its back. But don't imagine for one minute, boys, that they'd have let me go on working like that. I married my sawmill and my cornmill and got a couple of respectable daughters, and it's not done for Daddy to plough. It's not done for Daddy to tickle the girls and it's not done for Daddy to lie in the fields with his workers and eat the same meal. Damn it all, boys, nothing's done any longer as far as I'm concerned. But with you I can let my hair down. Listen, Jussi, here's a hundred marks for you. And one for you too, Kalle! And now we'll celebrate till the windows rattle. There'll be something for you, of course there's always something for you. There was that bathroom maid came and asked me to raise her wages because there wasn't enough for the kids. Of course I let her have it. Do you want more wages, boys, do you? But all they do at the sawmill is laugh and say I've had a drop too much. What business is that of theirs? Farmer Punttila gives and gives, because everybody must have it good, socialists, communists and the bourgeoisie. There's such a variety of us, we've got to get along together. Everyone can get along with Punttila.' And Punttila sang: '"Dear child, why sue me when you said/We always felt so close in bed?"

'You know, boys, why Punttila loves the entire world? The whole of humanity is good and nice. Have another coffee and schnapps. I shan't be able to take my sawmill and my steam mill and the estate into the grave with me, shall I? It's all got to stay here. Drink up, Jussi, drink, Kalle! We're all brothers in drink. There was a time when we fought to beat each other, and life was ugly, really ugly. But now it's possible to live again. The world is big enough, and there'll be enough for you and enough for farmer Punttila too. Cheers, Kalle!'

They went on cheerfully toping till the old housekeeper beckoned Kalle and Jussi into the back kitchen, after which Punttila again started mooching around, this time in the direction of the dining-room, which is two daughters at once left to dry their tears upstairs while Aunt Hanna went to the master of the house to ask for help.

In the dining-room Madam Maria waited for her guests, inwardly praying that they would sleep on until the Punttila problem had been painlessly deflected. To no effect. The English bank representative arrived first, since he was in the habit of getting up early despite the late night and the brandy.

When Aunt Hanna and her acolytes arrived back downstairs a strange performance greeted them. Beside the Englishman sat farmer Punttila, his hair unkempt, his face flushed by an inner dawn. He was alternately embracing the banker and embracing his bottle. At the end of the table sat Madam Maria telling the enchanged Englishman the story of Punttila's nocturnal escapades and how he had managed to get hold of his legal alcohol. Punttila patted the Englishman on the back and enthusiastically told him: 'You're just like a proper Finn, mate.'

The Englishman gave Punttila a friendly nod and laughed: 'A Finnish Bacchus!'

But Punttila thumped his barrel chest and asked: 'Did Maria go on to tell you that I threatened to smash all their hovels?'

In the golden morning light the silver shone, the cups clinked and old Fina in her snowy white apron poured coffee for Punttila and the bank director, while the village girl Selma handed round golden honey, jam and fragrant Finnish bread.

The Englishman approved heartily of what he saw of Fina, and said he couldn't stand those starchy English maids and menservants whom you had to address by their surnames. He envied his hostess.

        *   *   *

In their bedroom that evening, when the celebrations were all over, the young engineer was talking to his wife, Punttila's daughter: 'Did you notice the way Mother, the Englishmen, Fina and your father were winking at one another? I have a feeling, Toini, that it was a conspiracy of the more tolerant and civilised element against ourselves.'

Madam Toini gave a yawn: 'Rubbish. I could have sunk into the floor when I saw that schnapps bottle glinting on the table. You can't imagine what embarrassments my sister Martha and I have always had to undergo when in society.'

Toini was overwhelmed by self-pity.

In the next room slept farmer Punttila, who towards evening had grown sober and silent. He lay there on his own, full of resentment against Aunt Hanna, who had taken their hundred mark notes away from Jussi and Kalle. Next time Punttila was planning to give the lads two hundred marks apiece, and to do so under Aunt Hanna's nose.

[From *Brecht-Jahrbuch 1978*, edited by John Fuegi, Reinhold Grimm and Jost Hermand (Suhrkamp, Frankfurt, 1978, pp. 96 – 106). Translated into German from the original Finnish by Margareta N. Deschner]

Texts by Brecht

A NOTE OF 1940

The reader and, more important, the actor may be inclined to skim over passages such as the short dialogue between judge and lawyer (about the Finnish summer) in the sixth scene, because they use a homely way of speaking. However, the actor will not be performing the passage effectively unless he treats it as a prose poem, since it is one. Whether it is a good or a bad poem is not at this point relevant; the reader or actor can make up his own mind about that. The relevant thing is that it has to be treated as a poem, i.e., in a special manner, 'presented on a silver platter.' Matti's hymn of praise to the herring in scene 9 is an even better instance, perhaps. There is more than one situation in *Puntila* which would undoubtedly seem crude in a naturalistic play; for instance, any actor who plays the episode where Matti and Eva stage a compromising incident (scene 4) as if it were an episode from a farce will entirely fail to bring it off. This is exactly the kind of scene that calls for real virtuosity, as again do the tests to which Matti subjects his betrothed in scene 8. To cite the casket scene in *The Merchant of Venice* is not to propose any kind of qualitative comparison; though the scene may fall a long way short of Shakespeare's it can still only be made fully effective if one finds a way of acting something like that demanded by a verse play. Admittedly it is hard to speak of artistic simplicity rather than primitiveness when a play is written in prose and deals with 'ordinary' people. All the same the expulsion of the four village women (in scene 7) is not a primitive episode but a simple one, and as with the third scene (quest for legal alcohol and fiancées) it has to be played poetically; in other words the beauty of the episode (once again, be it big or be it small) must come across in the set, the movements, the verbal expression. The characters too have to be portrayed with a certain grandeur, and this again is something that will be none too easy for the actor who has only learnt to act naturalistically or fails to see that naturalistic acting is not enough in this case. It will help him if he realizes that it is his job to create a national character, and that this is going to call for all his sensitivity, daring, and knowledge of humanity. One last point: *Puntila* is far from being a play with a message. The Puntila part therefore must not for an instant be in any way deprived of its natural attractiveness, while particular artistry will be needed to make the drunk scenes delicate and poetic, with the maximum of variety, and the sober scenes as ungrotesque and unbrutal as possible. To put it in practical terms: Puntila has if possible to be staged in a style combining elements of the old commedia dell' arte and of the realistic play of mores.

[GW *Schriften zum Theater*, pp. 1167–8. This is the section bearing specifically on *Puntila* from the general essay 'Notes on the Folk Play' (or 'People's Play'), written in 1940, which will be included in Brecht's theatrical writings (and can meanwhile be found in *Brecht on Theatre*, pp. 153–7). It was originally prefaced by the words 'To take some instances from *Puntila*. . .']

NOTES ON THE ZURICH PREMIÈRE

1

Instead of the conventional curtain falling like a guillotine to chop the play into separate scenes, back to the lightly fluttering half-height linen curtain with the scene titles projected on it. During scene changes this curtain was somewhat lit so as to make it come to life and allow the audience to become more or less aware of the busy preparations being made for them on the stage. In particular they saw the upper parts of the big wall sections as they were shifted in, and they saw the sun's disc and the moon's sickle being lowered on wires, not yet illuminated and therefore visibly made of metal; they also saw the various little clouds being changed around.

2

These emblems for sun, moon, and clouds hung, like inn or shop signs, before the high broad wall of birch bark that constituted the background of the *Puntila* stage. According as to whether it was day, half-light, or night the wall was lit strongly, feebly, or not at all; the acting area being fully illuminated the while. In this way the atmospheric element was established in the background, independently of the rest of the performance.

3

No use was made of coloured light of any sort. Provided the lighting equipment is up to it the light should be as uniform as for a variety performance which includes the display of acrobatics. Sharply defined spotlighting would blot out the faces. Areas of darkness, even if only relative, detract from the words issuing from them. It is a good idea to have photographs taken to find out what kind of lighting is liable to strain the audience.

4

Colour and contrast can be supplied by the stage designer without having recourse to coloured light. The colour scheme for *Puntila* comprised blue, grey, and white for the stage, and black, grey, and white for the costumes. On top of this the latter were strictly realistic, with particular respect for details (the village women's handbags; the farm workers working barefoot on Sunday in their best trousers, shirts, and waistcoats, etc.).

5

All working processes must be shown in proper detail. (An actress who happened to have a child's figure turned Fina the maid into a memorable character by showing her working late at the washing (6), carrying butter (7) and falling asleep exhausted during Mr Puntila's engagement party (9).)

6

The permanent framework consisted of the great birch bark wall at the back already mentioned with thin structures of gold rods on either side downstage. The sets were composed of separate elements, those in the first scene for instance being (a) a wooden panelled wall with table, chairs, tablecloth covered with bottles of red wine, and a dozen empties grouped on the floor; and (b) a potted palm (the luxury element). Elements like those of the sixth scene, with its courtyard gateway and its main entrance to the house, could be definitively placed during the rehearsals. A further luxury element was a trashy plaster statuette in the second scene, whereas the slaughtered pig of scene 5, suspended from a scaffolding made of carmine-coloured joists and a brass rod, was no luxury element since it told of the preparations for the engagement banquet and was to be carried across the courtyard in the next scene. Importance was attached to the beauty and ease of the elements and the charm of their combination. At the same time they had to be realistic. Though the car in scene 3 consisted only of a truncated forepart it had been made from authentic components.

7

That the various stage elements, the costumes and the props should all look worn not only contributes to realism but also relieves the stage of that new, untested look.

8

Meaning, spatial dispositions, and colour must be such that every glimpse of the stage captures an image worth seeing.

9

The German language has no term for that aspect of mime which is known to the English stage as 'business', and we tend to introduce it half-heartedly, in an embarrassed way. Our word Kiste [literally, 'box'] which we use instead, shows the contempt in which it is held. All the same, Kisten [pieces of business] are essential components of narrative theatre. (*Puntila walks dryshod across the aquavit* (1); *Puntila hires a woodcutter because he likes his eyes* (4); *the women of Kurgela see butter, meat, and beer entering their fiancé's house* (7), and so on.) Such things were of course played for all they were worth. This was greatly helped by the 'one thing after another' principle, which any dramaturgy founded on exposition, climax, and thickening of the plot is always having to disregard.

10

The decisive point is the establishment of the class antagonism between Puntila and Matti. Matti must be so cast as to bring about a true balance, i.e., so as to give him intellectually the upper hand. The actor playing Puntila must be careful not to let his vitality or charm in the drunk scenes so win over the audience that they are no longer free to look at him critically.

11

Among the play's nobler characters are the four women from Kurgela. It would be completely wrong to portray them as comic; rather they are full of humour. They would anyway have to be attractive, if only because their expulsion must be attributable to no other cause then their inferior status.

12

Possible cuts: Scene 4 (The Hiring Fair) is deleted. But parts of it are used in the following scene (Scandal at Puntila Hall).

Then scene 5 begins as follows:

The yard at Puntila Hall. A bath-hut, the interior of which is visible. Forenoon. Over the door leading into the house Laina the cook and Fina the maid are nailing a sign saying 'Welcome to the Engagement Party!'

Puntila and Matti come in through the gate, followed by a few workers.

LAINA: Welcome back. Miss Eva and His Excellency and His Honour are here, and they're all having breakfast.

PUNTILA: First thing I want to know is what's the matter with Surkkala. Why is he packing?

LAINA: You promised the parson you'd get rid of him because he's a Red.

PUNTILA: What, Surkkala? The only intelligent tenant I've got? Besides, he has four children. What must he think of me? Parson be buggered, I'll forbid him the house for his inhumanity. Send Surkkala here right away, I want to apologise to him and his family. Send the children too, all four of them, so I can express my personal regret for the fear and insecurity they must have been through.

LAINA: No call for that, Mr Puntila.

PUNTILA, *seriously*: Oh yes there is. *Pointing to the workers*: These gentlemen are staying. Get them all an aquavit, Laina. I'm taking them on to work in the forest.

LAINA: I thought you were selling the forest.

PUNTILA: Me? I'm not selling any forest. My daughter's got her dowry between her legs, right? And I've brought these men home because I can't stand those hiring fairs. If I want to buy a horse or a cow I'll go to a fair without thinking twice about it. But you're human beings, and it's not right for human beings to be bargained over in a market. Am I right?

THE WEEDY MAN: Absolutely.

MATTI: Excuse me, Mr Puntila, but you're not right. They want work and you've got work, and whether it's done at a fair or in church it's still buying and selling.

PUNTILA: Brother, would you inspect me to see if my feet are crooked, the way you inspect a horse's teeth?

MATTI: No. I'd take you on trust.

PUNTILA, *indicating the weedy-looking man*: That fellow wouldn't be bad. I like the look in his eye.

MATTI: Mr Puntila, I don't want to speak out of turn, but that man's no use to you, he'll never be able to stand it.

THE WEEDY MAN: Here, I like that. What tells you I'll never be able to stand it?

MATTI: An eleven-and-a-half-hour day in summer. It's just that I don't want to see you let down, Mr Puntila. You'll only have to throw him out when he cracks up.

PUNTILA: I'm going into the sauna. Tell Fina to bring me some coffee. While I'm undressing you go and fetch two or three more so I can take my pick.

He goes into the bath hut and undresses, Fina brings the workers aquavit.

MATTI, *to Fina*: Get him some coffee.

THE RED-HEADED MAN: What's it like up at Puntila Hall?

MATTI: So-so. Four quarts of milk. Milk's good. You get potatoes too, I'm told. Room's on the small side.

THE RED-HEADED MAN: How far's school? I've got a little girl.

MATTI: About an hour's walk.

THE RED-HEADED MAN: That's nothing in fine weather. What's he like?

MATTI: Too familiar. It won't matter to you, you'll be in the forest, but I'm with him in the car, I can't get away from him and before I know where I am he's turning all human on me. I can't take it much longer.

Surkkala comes in with his four children.

MATTI: Surkkala! For God's sake clear off right away. Once he's had his bath and knocked back his coffee, he'll be stone cold sober and better look out if he catches you around the yard. Take my advice, you'll keep out of his sight the next day or two.

Surkkala nods and is about to hasten away with the children.

PUNTILA, *who has undressed and listened but failed to hear the end of this, peers out of the bath hut and observes Surkkala and the children*: Surkkala! I'll be with you in a moment. *To Matti*: Give him ten marks earnest money.

MATTI: Yes, but can't you make up your mind about this lot? They'll miss the hiring fair.

PUNTILA: Don't rush me. I don't buy human beings in cold blood. I'm offering them a home on the Puntila estate.

THE RED-HEADED MAN: Then I'm off. I need a job. *He goes.*

PUNTILA: Stop! He's gone. I could have used him. *To the weedy man*: Don't let him put you off. You'll do the work all right. I give you my word of honour. You understand what that means, the word of a Tavastland farmer? Mount Hatelma can crumble, it's not very likely but it can, but the word of a Tavastland farmer stands for ever, everyone knows that. *To Matti*: Come inside, I need you to pour the water over me. *To the weedy man*: You can come in too.

(Unchanged from p. 32, line 8 to p. 35, line 16. Then:)

PUNTILA, *to Fina*: Now this is what I've decided, and I want you to listen so what I say doesn't get twisted around later as it usually does. *Indicating one of the labourers*: I'd have taken that one, but his trousers are too posh for me, he's not going to strain himself. Clothes are the thing to look out for: too good means he thinks he's too good to work, too torn means he's got a bad character. It's all right for a gardener, for instance, to go around in patched trousers so long as it's the knees are patched, not the seat, yes, with a gardener it has to be the knees. I only need one look to see what's a man's made of, his age doesn't matter, if he's old he'll carry as much or more because he's frightened of being turned off, what I go by is the man himself. Intelligence is no use to me, that lot spend all day totting up their hours of work. I don't like that, I'd sooner be on friendly terms with my men. *To a strongly built labourer*: You can come along, I'll give you your earnest money inside. And that reminds me. *To Matti, who has emerged from the bath hut*: Give me your jacket. You're to hand over your jacket, d'you hear? *He is handed Matti's jacket.* Got you boyo. *Shows him the wallet*: What do I find in your pocket? Had a feeling about you, spotted you for an old lag first go off. Is that my wallet or isn't it?

MATTI: Yes, Mr Puntila.

PUNTILA: Now you're for it, ten years' gaol, all I have to do is ring the police.

MATTI: Yes, Mr Puntila.

PUNTILA: But that's a favour I'm not doing you. So you can lead the life of Riley in a cell, lying around and eating the taxpayer's bread, what? That'd suit you down to the ground. At harvest time too. So you'd get out of driving the tractor. But I'm putting it all down in your reference, you get me?

MATTI: Yes, Mr Puntila

Puntila walks angrily towards the house. On the threshold stands Eva, carrying her straw hat. She has been listening.

THE WEEDY MAN: Should I come along then, Mr Puntila?

PUNTILA: You're no use to me whatever, you'll never stand it.

THE WEEDY MAN: But the hiring fair's over now.

PUNTILA: You should have thought of that sooner instead of trying to take advantage of my friendly mood. I remember exactly who takes advantage of it. *To the labourer who has followed him*: I've thought it over and I'm taking nobody at all. I'll probably sell the forest, and you can blame it on him there [*he points at Matti*] for deliberately leaving me in the dark about something I needed to know, the bastard. I'll show him. *Exit into the house, brooding*.

(Then unchanged from p. 36, line 13 on.)

[GW *Schriften zum Theater*, pp. 1169–73, and GW *Stücke*, pp. 1713–17, which originally were consecutive. Written in 1948 and first published in *Versuche 10*, 1950. For the Zurich première of June 5, 1948, the scene designer was Teo Otto. Puntila was played by Leonard Steckel, Matti by Gustav Knuth.]

NOTES ON THE BERLINER ENSEMBLE PRODUCTION

1. Prologues, inter-scene songs, and scene titles

Our new audience, being engaged in building a new life for itself, insists on having its say and not just accepting what happens on the stage ('That's how things are and what's to change them?'); it doesn't like having to guess the playwright's viewpoint. Prologues, songs during scene changes, and the occasional projection of scene titles on the half-curtain all make for direct contact with the audience. The actress playing the dairymaid, Regine Lutz, delivered a short verse prologue with a bunch of everlastings in her hand. For the Zurich production there were scene titles [examples as in our text are cited]. Prologues are to be found in the classic drama, scene titles however only in the classic adventure story. They put the audience in a state of mild suspense and lead it to look for something definite in the scene that follows. In the Berliner Ensemble production the scene titles were dropped in favour of the singing of the Puntila song. Annemarie Hase, playing the cook, stepped before the curtain carrying whatever household utensils she happened to be working with, thus making it possible to follow the various stages of the great Puntila engagement party. Her song was accompanied on the other side of the stage by two musicians who had appeared before the curtain carrying a guitar and a piano accordion. The song gave a running commentary on events at Puntila Hall as viewed from the kitchen, and by making them celebrated as it were, turned Mr Puntila's escapades into aspects of local history.

2. Some principles of the production illustrated

This play's satire is of a poetic kind. The director's task therefore is to translate its poetic features into memorable images.

At the beginning of the play, for instance, we encounter a Puntila of almost mythological grandeur. He is the triumphant last survivor of a veritable flood of spirituous liquors, in which all his drinking companions have drowned. [. . .]

The director accordingly must conjure up Puntila's moan of isolation and his berating of the inadequate judge; Puntila's encounter with a human being (Puntila is on the dining table demonstrating how one walks across a sea of aquavit when he catches sight of Matti. He has to clamber down and steer a wide course round the gratuitously large table in order to greet Matti and bring him back to the table); the revealing of his dreadful malady (Puntila formally creeps into the protesting Matti); Matti's ghost story (while he eats he recalls those who are being starved on the big landed estates); Puntila promoting Matti to be a friend and then consulting him about his own personal affairs (to solve his shabby problems Puntila keeps Matti up when he would much rather go home and go to bed); Matti leading a subdued Puntila out of the hotel (again a wide tour of the table, Puntila having confidingly and ceremoniously handed him the wallet containing his despised money).

3. The way people work

Showing how work is actually done is something the bourgeois theatre finds uninteresting; the usual solution is to botch up any old thing. It is essential that Matti, the chauffeur, should work deftly, whether he is changing a tyre as he talks to the landowner's daughter, or sweeping out the yard, or massaging Puntila, or dragging out the drunken judge. Likewise the kitchenmaid's serving of coffee, soaking of linen, and carrying of butter all have to be got right.

4. Puntila's drunkenness

The actor playing Puntila will find that his chief problem is how to portray the drunkenness which makes up 90 per cent of the part. It would seem unacceptably repellent were he to contribute the conventional drunk act, in other words to demonstrate a state of intoxication blurring over and devaluing every physical and mental process. The drunkenness played by Steckel was the drunkenness specific to Puntila, i.e. that through which the landowner achieves his semblance of humanity. Far from exhibiting the usual impairments of speech and physical movement, he displayed a rhythmical, almost musical way of speaking and relaxed, almost ballet-like movements. Admittedly a certain handicap was imposed on his inspiration by the weight of his limbs, which was too great for those superterrestrial motions which he had in mind. He ascended Mount Hatelma on wings, albeit slightly defective ones. Each of the monster's drunken gests – of meekness, anger at injustice, generosity in giving and taking, comradeship, and what not – was developed with gusto. Puntila abandoned his possessions like a Buddha, disowned his daughter as in the Bible, invited the Kurgela women to be his guests like some Homeric monarch.

5. Steckel's two Puntilas

Before playing Puntila in Berlin Steckel had played him in Zurich. There he played almost without makeup, and the impression gained by most of the audience was of a likeable man subject to the occasional nasty turn when in a state of sobriety, which state being tantamount to a hangover the turns seemed excusable. In Berlin, in view of these effects, he opted for a foully shaped bald head and made himself up with debauched and debased features. Only now did his drunken charm seem menacing and his sociable approaches like those of a crocodile. Nearly all German performances of this play, whether before or after the Berlin production, suffered from the same mistake as was made in Zurich.

6. Socially based humour

There is little that a play like *Puntila* can take from the rag-bag of 'timeless humour.' True, even in 'timeless humour' there is a social element – the clown sets out brimming with self-confidence and falls flat on his face – but it has become overlaid to the point where the clown's fall appears like something purely biological, something that is humorous to all people under all conditions. The actors who perform *Mr Puntila and his Man Matti* must derive their humour from the prevailing class situation, even if that means there are one or two classes whose members will not laugh. When the happily reintoxicated landowner gets Matti to build him a Mount Hatelma from the billiard-room furniture, Matti does so with anger, because even in the depths of drunkenness Puntila did not omit to sack Red Surkkala. Relentlessly he demolishes gun cabinet and grandfather clock; this is going to be an expensive mountain. At each crash Puntila winces and his smile becomes forced.– In the village Puntila listens to the life stories of the Kurgela girls, but he does not listen properly because he knows what is coming and takes a long pull of 'legal alcohol' after every story. The humour is of a gloomy sort.– If the landowner takes the women's 'Plum' song as a personal tribute that is traditional humour and unexceptionable. But there is added depth if he appears somehow interested in folklore and adopts a knowledgeable expression. It shows up the cleft which is the theme of the play.– In scene 4 Puntila brings a group of agricultural workers back from the hiring fair. It is the one day in the year when they are able to find jobs, and Puntila has no use for them; he just wants company. He at once raises one man's hopes ('I like the look in his eye'). Then he breaks through the ring of workers surrounding him and hastens into the sauna in order to sober up enough to get the strength to throw the workers out. The cravenness of this flight into sobriety is a stroke of humour that can scarcely be achieved except by an actor with social understanding and socialist principles.

7. The women of Kurgela

From the outset the portrayal of those women of Kurgela whom Puntila invites to his estate when drunk and throws out when sober presented great problems. These are the noblest characters in the play, and in planning their costumes and makeup we hestitated a long time between the beautiful and the characteristic before realising that these are not really opposites. To give a fairy-tale quality to the story of the four early risers we started by making stylised costumes with very delicate colours, then thought them boring and plumped for naturalism without regard for beauty. This led to outsize boots and long noses. Then Caspar Neher intervened. Full of scepticism, he came to the rehearsals and produced a batch of scene designs that are among the most beautiful things which our generation has created for the theatre. He solved the problem of how to reconcile the women's naïve behaviour with their practical worldly wisdom by having them play a light-hearted game with the landowner. With jokes and a bit of play-acting they confronted the landowner as a body, as the legendary 'Women of Kurgela', biblical brides hoping for a dance and a coffee from their bridegroom on high. Neher made them don straw garlands, and he endowed the chauffeur Matti too with imagination, devising the broom which he sticks in the ground and addresses as the High Court at Viborg, and also uses to sweep up the garlands when they have thrown them down in the yard following their unpleasant reception. Now that their behaviour had been got right there was virtually no problem in making the costumes and makeup beautiful. The cut of the costumes remained realistic, but their contours were somewhat stressed and identical material was used for all of them. The faces were given a certain uncouth, peasant quality – we began by testing the effect of crumbled cement which we tried out on plaster casts – while a golden complexion was created by covering them with warm-toned pounded ochre. The big shoes, retained for one of the women, in no way detracted from the beauty which came above all from the dignity of these working women. Starting as poor guests, they became rich in kindliness, ready and willing to bestow their humour even on a landowner; from poetic figures they turned into real people with a feeling for poetry. Composed by a great painter, the groupings lent grace and power to their natural, realistic demeanour.

8.   Caspar Neher's Puntila stage

The symbolist stage of Expressionists and Existentialists, which expresses general ideas, is of no use to a realistic theatre, nor can we go back to the naturalistic stage with its crude mixture of the relevant and the irrelevant. A mere echo of the real world is not enough; it must be not only recognisable but also understandable. This means that the images have to be artistically valid and to display an individual handwriting. Wit and imagination are specially desirable in the designer of a comedy.

9.   The masks

Puntila, the Attaché, the parson, parson's wife, lawyer, and judge all wore more or less grotesque masks and moved in a foolish, regal manner. Matti, the women of Kurgela, the hired hands, and the agricultural workers wore no masks and moved normally. An exception was made for Eva, the landowner's daughter; she had no mask. Any suggestion that this amounts to symbolism would be unfounded. No hidden significance is intended. The theatre is simply adopting an attitude and heightening significant aspects of reality, to wit, certain physiognomical malformations to be found in parasites.

10. Is a play like *Mr Puntila and his Man Matti* still relevant to us now that the big estates have been got rid of?

There is an attractive kind of impatience which would have the theatre only present things in their current real-life state. Why waste time on an estate owner? Haven't we got rid of such people? Why show a proletarian like Matti? Don't we have more active fighters? Likeable as such impatience is, it should not be given way to. The fact that alongside those works of art which we have to organise there are certain works of art that have come down to us is only a valid argument if the usefulness of the latter can be proved, never mind how much time is needed to organise the former. Why can *Mr Puntila and his Man Matti* still be regarded as a play with relevance? Because not only the struggle but the history of that struggle is instructive. Because past eras leave a deposit in people's souls for a long time. Because the class struggle demands that victory in one area of conflict be exploited so as to promote victory in another, and in both cases the situation prior to victory may be similar. Because, like all pioneers, people who have been liberated from their oppressors may at first have a hard life, since they have to replace the oppressors' system with a new one. These are the sorts of arguments that can be adduced to show the relevance of plays like *Mr Puntila and his Man Matti*.

[1. 4 and 10 from GW SzT 1173–5, the rest from pp. 18–45 of *Theaterarbeit* (1950), for which these notes were written. They refer to the Berliner Ensemble production of 1949, in which Puntila was played initially by Steckel once more, and later by the comedian Curt Bois. Paul Dessau's setting of the songs was written for this. The last note is an answer to some of Brecht's East German critics.]

NOTES ON THE PUNTILA FILM

1. About the script for *Puntila*

As it stands the script doesn't seem right to me. It is true that it follows
the general line which Pozner and I agreed on, but in the course of
its realisation the story has lapsed into a genre which makes it not so
much comic as ridiculous. It has become a drawing-room comedy in
which the crude jokes of the play jar and seem merely crude. Nor is
it clear *who* is telling the entire story or from what point of view. The
film company, it would seem, and from the point of view of making
a film. The Puntila tales have of course to be told from below, from
the position of the people. Then characters like Matti and Eva Puntila
can be seen in the right light. The present script turns Matti into a
feeble, indefinite figure; it fails to bring out how despite and because
of their master/man relationship he is in continual opposition to his
employer in every line he says. What makes Eva Puntila 'love' him is
not his muscles – it would be all the same if he had none – but the fact
that he is a proper man, humorous, dominating and so forth. Nor of
course must he for one instant imagine that Eva is the right wife for
him or that Mr Puntila would really let him have her. His *test* is simply
a way of deflating Eva and Puntila's romantic notion. It has to remain
a game if Matti is not to be made into an idiot.

We have made a new outline, since I realise that the studio cannot
wait. As the poetic material is already at hand the preparation of a new
shooting script would be a remarkably quick business. Given the
script as it is I would find it quite impossible to turn the new dialogue
(which makes up at least half the total dialogue and is entirely
naturalistic) into Puntila-German, because the situations are
naturalistic and in my view false. Nor if this script were used could
I under any circumstances allow the use of my name or the name
Puntila. I am not by any means out to make difficulties, but neither
do I wish to damage my reputation as a writer. I am sure you will
understand this.

2. New story line for *Puntila*

1. Hotel Tavasthus

Surrounded by passed-out drunks and dead-tired waiters, a man is
traversing a vast table covered with plates of meat and bottles: it is Mr

Puntila. He claims to be able to walk dry-shod across the sea of aquavit represented to him by the table top. Another man addresses him, and turns out to be his chauffeur whom he has left waiting outside for two days and a night. Feeling lonely and abandoned by his too easily intoxicated friends – the judge, the teacher, and so on – Puntila instantly becomes bosom pals with his chauffeur Matti and discusses with him his most intimate concerns, i.e. his daughter Eva's forthcoming engagement to an attaché. For this a dowry is required, so he must sell a forest. To postpone the decision Puntila has got drunk. They decide to have another look at the forest.

2. Forest

Puntila realises that the forest is too beautiful to sell. Sooner than that he will marry Widow Klinckmann, who is rich and the owner of the Kurgela estate, but whom he last saw fifty years ago. Off to Kurgela.

3. Kurgela

Rousing the sleepy domestics Puntila pushes his way through them into Widow Klinckmann's bedroom. One look is enough: the widow is too hideous to sell himself to.

4. The Village of Kurgela Next Day

Fleeing from Widow Klinckmann and avid for beauty, Puntila meets three young women, is upset by the sadness of their lives and instantly becomes engaged to them. He tells them to come to Puntila Hall on the following Sunday. The young women take this as a jest on the part of a well-to-do drunk gentleman, and laughingly promise they will come. The telephone operator, last of the three, advises him to drive to the hiring fair at Lammi, where he will meet another estate owner called Bibelius who wants to buy his forest. He will recognise him by his butterfly tie-pin. Since the forest has to be sold after all, Puntila decides to drive to Lammi.

5. Hiring Fair

The alcoholic effects are wearing off. Puntila gives vent to some intelligent and ill-natured remarks about servants. Drinks coffee laced with rum, and apologises to Matti. Discloses his malady and asks Matti for moral support. Engages four cripples because he likes them as people. Sees a fat man beating a horse and tells him where to get off. On Matti and the workers expressing their enthusiastic approval he learns that he has just beaten up the man who wants to buy his forest. This sobers him up, and he gets gloomily into his car without offering a lift to the labourers.

'Home,' he says curtly. 'I'm selling the forest to Widow Klinckmann.'

6. Puntila Hall

Preparations for the engagement party are in full swing. Pigs are being slaughtered, windows cleaned, and Matti is helping the cook to nail up a garlanded sign which says 'Welcome to the Engagement Party.' Miss Puntila would like to know what Matti thinks of her engagement to the Attaché. She herself has no use for him. With considerable ingenuity she induces Matti to help her stage a scandal in order to frighten off the Attaché, who is now staying at Puntila Hall. The scandal is staged (sauna) but clearly the Attaché must have enormous debts: he overlooks it. Puntila is very angry, takes his wallet from Matti, and threatens to tell the police. Eva blames Matti for not sticking up for himself like a gentleman.

7. Summer Nights in Tavastland

The combination of the feigned love scene with Matti and the erotic ambience of the summer night has put fresh thoughts into Eva's head. On the pretext of catching crayfish she takes Matti rowing to a somewhat notorious island. Once there however the thought that she is behaving like a milkmaid disconcerts her; she insists on catching crayfish and is eventually rowed back by a frustrated Matti.

8. Puntila Hall

Puntila turns his three 'fiancées' off the estate, then tells Matti to collect the entire stock of liquor so that it can be destroyed. Thousands of bottles are collected in an operation involving the entire staff. Puntila drinks extravagantly and sends Matti off to bring back his 'fiancées'. Beaming, he announces that in his view they are much better suited than certain other people to the sort of engagement party he has in mind.

9. Country Road

Matti drives off after the young women, but fails to persuade them to return.

10. Inside Puntila Hall

All the guests have arrived, including the foreign minister. Eva has locked herself in her room, so that the Attaché has to receive them on his own. Enter like a whirlwind a totally drunk Puntila, who throws the Attaché out. Thereafter he throws out the minister, parson, judge, and so on, and sends for the domestics. Matti on his return is offered Eva as his wife. Matti insists on testing Eva's matrimonial capacities. She shows herself incompetent to do her own housework. Eventually when Matti slaps her on the backside she takes it badly and runs off in tears. Left alone, Puntila hears his hired hands singing the Ballad of the Forester and the Countess. He resolves to show Matti what a beautiful country they live in, and with this object they climb Mount Hatelma.

11. In the Yard

Matti turns his back on Puntila.

[Brecht: *Texte für Filme II*, Frankfurt, Suhrkamp, 1969, pp. 636–40. The Puntila film, under the same title as the play, was made in Austria by Wien-Film with Alberto Cavalcanti as director and Curt Bois in the title part (which he had also played in the second Berliner Ensemble production), and was first shown in Brussels on March 29, 1955. Vladimir Pozner was one of the scriptwriters. A new musical score was written by Hanns Eisler, and the text of the Puntila Song somewhat varied for the purpose.]

Editorial Note

1. PRELIMINARY IDEAS

Though the Puntila theme was not Brecht's own it none the less struck several familiar chords in his mind, among them being Faustian Man (with his twin souls), Chaplin's film *City Lights*, and the ironic discursive style of Hašek's *Schweik*. They may well moreover (as Jost Hermand has suggested) have included Carl Zuckmayer's bucolic 'People's Play' of 1925, *Der fröhliche Weinberg* (The Cheerful Vineyard), and the falsely jovial personality of Reichsmarschall Hermann Göring. There is, however, no sign of such elements coming together before Brecht met Hella Wuolijoki in 1940. Stimulated, so it appears, by the Finnish Dramatists' League's play competition, she then showed him her play *The Sawdust Princess* together with the film treatment from which it derived, with the result that by August 27 they had agreed to collaborate on a new version. For her the theme went back to the early 1930s when (according to evidence gathered by Hans-Peter Neureuter in the *Mitteilungen aus der deutschen Bibliothek*, Helsinki, numbers 7, 1973 and 8, 1974), she wrote the story based on the personality of one of her own relatives, which she called 'A Finnish Bacchus'. This was worked up into a treatment for Suomi-Film, which however was never made. Its central character, says Margaret Mare in her edition of the play (Methuen, 1962), was to be

Puntila, a Tavastland estate owner, who, mellowed by drink, went one night to the village and engaged himself to several young women with the help of liquor and curtain rings. Puntila has a daughter, Eva . . . who is wooed both by a young diplomat and by a chauffeur. She chooses the latter, and all ends well when he turns out to be an engineer, masquerading in his own chauffeur's uniform.

Puntila himself was to marry 'Aunt Hanna', the owner of the house where he arrives drunk early in the story (and where he also confronts his village 'fiancées').

How far the play *The Sawdust Princess* was complete when Brecht first saw it is not entirely clear. Some commentators think that it was, but Brecht himself referred to it as a draft and in his journal (entry for September 2) describes it thus:

> hw's half-finished play is a comedy, a conversation piece. (puntila sober is puntila drunk plus a hangover, hence in a bad temper, the stereotype of a drinker. his chauffeur is a *gentleman* who had applied for the chauffeur's job after having seen a photograph of puntila's daughter, etc.) but there is also a film of hers which yields some useful epic elements (the mountain climb and the trip for legal alcohol). it is my job to bring out the underlying farce, dismantle the psychologically-orientated conversations, make room for opinions and for stories from finnish popular life, find scenic terms for the master/servant antithesis, and restore the poetry and comedy proper to this theme.

This was not, of course, the job as Hella Wuolijoki herself saw it, but in Brecht's view she was handicapped by a hopelessly conventional dramatic technique. A fortnight before, he had already tried to give her an idea of 'non-Aristotelian' dramaturgy while discussing a plan of hers to write a play about the early Finnish nationalist J. V. Snellman, a work which she never completed. Now he took over *The Sawdust Princess* and within three weeks had turned it into something very different from what he had found.

He started with a German translation which Wuolijoki, an excellent linguist, dictated to Margarete Steffin. From this orthodox four-act play he took the characters of Puntila, Eva (the Sawdust Princess of the title), the Attaché, the doctor, Fina the maid, and all the village women apart from the chemist's assistant. Initially he also took Kalle the pseudo-chauffeur, whom he turned into a genuine chauffeur and later renamed Matti, while from the treatment he took Aunt Hanna, first turning her into Puntila's housekeeper, then banishing her from the play altogether except in the shadowy form of the unseen Mrs Klinckmann. The setting and the Swedish-style place names – Tavastland or Häme in southwest Finland, Kurgela, Lammi, Tammerfors (Tampere), Mount Hatelma (Hattelmala near Tavasthus) and so on – are likewise taken from Wuolijoki, Kurgela indeed being the nearest sizeable town to her own Marlebäck estate.

A succession of plans shows Brecht isolating the crucial incidents in her story, switching them and building on them until he had the framework of a ten-scene play. One of the earliest gives Puntila the aristocratic 'von' and goes thus:

1. Mr von P. gets engaged to the churchgoers.
2. The league of Mr von P.'s fiancées.
3. Playing with fire (those who pretend to be in love fall in love).
4. Driving out the materialists.
5. Mr von P. sits in judgement.
6.
7. Climbing the mountain.
8. Mr von P.'s funeral speech.

Thereafter (it would seem) two new scenes were added at the start (the first being described as 'gethsemane/a chauffeur with dignity/the engagement'), while the centre of the play was left undetermined. According as to whether Puntila was to be mainly drunk or sober, Brecht now started marking the scenes 'd' or 's' – that is, in German 'b' or 'n', b(esoffen) or n(üchtern). Kalle's new role became clearer and something like the final play began to take shape:

1. puntila finds a human being and hires him as his chauffeur (d).
2.
3. puntila finds legal alcohol and gets engaged to the early risers. (d).
4. p engages his daughter to a human being/in the sauna/the league of mr von p's fiancées/kalle and eva conduct a test. (d and s).
5. p engages his daughter to an attaché/the attaché is uncongenial to him/k refuses to marry eva/puntila rejects her. (s and d).
6. judgement on kalle/kalle says goodbye to e/the mountain climb.
7. k leaves p and makes a speech about him.

Next the two main events of this scene 4, the engagement and the league of fiancées, are separated, the former being shifted to a separate scene immediately before or after scene 5. One scheme introduces 'p gets engaged to his housekeeper' as the theme of the last scene but one. Finally there is a characteristic big working plan in columns, such as Brecht used to pin up before starting to write in earnest:

1. p finds a human being.
2. p and his daughter.
3. p gets engaged to the early risers.
4. p engages his daughter to an attaché.
5. p at the hiring market.
6. kalle goes on strike.
7. the league of p's fiancées.
8. p engages his daughter to a human being.
9. p sits in judgement and climbs mount hatelma.
10. kalle turns his back on p.

Though two further scenes were to be added, initially as 7a and 8a, while 9 and 10 became run together, the above is in effect the play as Brecht first wrote it. He also kept before him three examples of what he called 'Puntila's way of speaking' (the passage starting 'I'd be ashamed', p. 40), 'Kalle's way of speaking' (a passage in scene 6 starting 'Your father's acting all for your best', p. 49), and 'the gentry's way of speaking' (the judge's passage in the same scene starting 'All those paternity cases', p. 45). Once these tones of voice had been fixed 'the work went very smoothly,' he noted, even though the tone was not original:

it is hašek's way of speaking in schweik, as already used by me in courage. the plan for the scenes was quickly settled. their length was predetermined and fairly closely kept to. the visit to the hiring fair was an afterthought; it took place a few days ago near here.

So he wrote in his journal on September 19, the day when he had finished the play and handed it to Hella Wuolijoki to read.

At first her reactions were far from favourable. 'She seems

extremely alarmed', says a journal entry five days later:

> it is undramatic, unfunny, etc. all the characters speak alike, not
> differently as they do in real life and in hw's plays. passages like the
> conversation between judge and lawyer in the kitchen are boring
> (something the finns are not unused to) and do nothing to further
> the plot. Kalle is not a finnish chauffeur. the landowner's daughter
> cannot attempt to borrow money from the chauffeur (but can
> presumably attempt to marry him, as in hw's play): it's all so epic
> as to be undramatic.

Brecht tried to encourage her, not least because she still had to
produce a Finnish text for submission to the jury. Though she
accepted something of what he said,

> the point i could not get across was that my scenes' gait and garb
> corresponded to the gait and garb of puntila himself, with all his
> aimlessness, looseness, his detours and delays, his repetitions and
> improprieties. she wants to bring on the women of kurgela earlier,
> immediately they have been invited, so as to make sure the audience
> has not forgotten them. she fails to see the beauty of having them
> virtually forgotten, not only by the audience but by puntila too,
> then making them pop up long after the morning of the invitation.

None the less she did embark on the translation, and only ten days
later seemed very happy about the whole undertaking. She told Brecht
(who again noted it in his journal) that the play was full of riches and
Puntila himself on the way to becoming 'a national figure'.

In the Finnish version published in 1946 (by Tammi of Helsinki)
the name Puntila is changed to Iso-Heikkilä and the title of the play
to *The Landowner Iso-Heikkilä and His Servant Kalle*, subtitled 'A
comic tale of Tavastland drunkenness in nine scenes' by Hella
Wuolijoki and Bertolt Brecht. An introductory note stresses this
aspect:

> Iso-Heikkilä's intoxication is in the nature of a divine dionysiac
> drunkenness. As a steadfast man of Tavastland, he never falters –
> an inner radiance like the brightness of early morning and an always
> human kindness and strength shine forth from his face. Alcohol is

only the magic potion which releases all the sources of kindness in the man, the landowner, Iso-Heikkilä.

'The structure,' she wrote, 'is entirely Brecht's. The idea of including epic tales in the scenes with the women was Brecht's. The stories themselves are entirely mine.' The change of name apart, this version is very close to Brecht's own first typescript dated '2.9.40–19.9.40 (Marlebäck)', though the latter also seems to include some later amendments. Then entitled simply *Puntila*, it was retyped by Margarete Steffin and given its final title; mimeographed copies were thereafter made and sent out by Reiss of Basel. Up to this point there were no songs embodied in the play, though those of Red Surkkala and Emma have been appended to the retyped copy, the former as an alternative to 'The wolf asked the rooster' (pp. 146–147 below). Then it was revised again after the Zurich première in 1948, when changes were made for Brecht's own production with Erich Engel for the Berliner Ensemble, the Puntila Song being written as late as 1949. Around that time the Munich publisher Kurt Desch acquired the stage rights, but at first he too simply duplicated the nine-scene version, which was described as 'after Hella Wuolijoki's stories' with no mention of her play; she is not named as co-author in any of the German texts, though Brecht in 1949 told Desch that she was to get half the royalties.

By 1950, when Suhrkamp first published the text (as *Versuche 10*), the play had expanded from the nine scenes of the early versions – or ten in those scripts where the epilogue was counted separately – to the present twelve. From the first, however, it included the scene with the hiring fair which had only figured in the last of the plans. The character of Surkkala introduced there was subsequently built up, being alluded to at various points and making a notable appearance also in scene 11. Like the village women's accounts of their lives in scene 3, their 'Finnish tales' in scene 8 were an evident afterthought on Brecht's first script, those now given to Emma being omitted from the 1946 Finnish version, possibly because of the censorship. As Aunt Hanna's role diminished from landowner to housekeeper (shedding the 'Aunt') and finally to nothing at all, around the end of the 1940s the shadowy Mrs Klinckmann was introduced to perform some of her original functions, and various references to Puntila's marrying her or selling the forest worked in. Meanwhile in the joint Finnish version

Hella Wuolijoki had given the Attaché an uncle to be the owner of Kurgela and speak some of the lines now given to the lawyer. The Kurgela location still survives in the play, even though without the aunt or uncle most of its *raison d'être* disappeared, its main bath-hut episode being shifted to Puntila Hall and run together with the sobering-up operation to form the present scene 5. Finally there was a change of balance in the relationship between Eva and Matti (Kalle), which Wuolijoki seems to have wanted still to treat as a conventional love story destined for a happy ending (see the last scene of the 1946 Finnish version). Something of her interpretation can be detected even in the first Brecht scripts (as in the detailed account of scene 9 below), a greater element of ambiguity and coolness being introduced later. Throughout, the unchanging pillars of the play were the first half of scene 1, scene 3, the bath-hut episode in scene 5, Matti's dialogue with Eva in scene 6, scenes 7 and 9, and the mountain-climbing episode in scene 11.

The detailed notes which follow are based on comparison of Brecht's first script (1940), the fair copy (1940–41), the joint Wuolijoki–Brecht version (published 1946), the *Versuche* text (1950), and the final text as we have it. Changes made for the Zurich production of 1948 are separately dealt with in Brecht's own note on pp. 114–117.

2. SCENE-BY-SCENE ACCOUNT
Cast

The first script includes the housekeeper Hanna and a doctor, has a peasant woman in lieu of Emma, and omits Surkkala and his children. The chauffeur is still Kalle, but becomes Matti on the fair copy. In the Wuolijoki–Brecht version of 1946 (which we will call the W–B version) Puntila is Johannes Iso-Heikkilä and his housekeeper is called Alina. There is an 'Agronomist Kurgela, a relative of Iso-Heikkilä's, owner of the Kurgela estate', while the attaché is 'Ilmari Silakkala, Kurgela's nephew, a foreign ministry official'. A note to the W–B version says: 'This all took place when Tavastland was still a cheerful place without a single war refugee.'

Prologue

In the first script this is spoken by Kalle and omits eight lines in the middle. The W–B version has it delivered before the curtain by the whole cast and considerably alters the general sense. This is to the effect that a bad time can be expected in Finland, but one has to be able to laugh all the same. So the audience is invited to appreciate human character and take part in the wild excursions of master and man: never mind if the humour is broad and the element of mockery strong; the actors' work is only play. 'This drama was written in praise of Tavastland and its people.'

In the 1950 text the opening couplet went 'Ladies and gentlemen, the times are bad / When worry's sane and not to worry mad.' The present, slightly more optimistic version first appeared in 1952.

Scene 1

Brecht's original idea, which he amended in the first script, was to set the scene in a village tavern, with a landlord rather than a waiter. In the W–B version Iso-Heikkilä (whom we shall call Puntila for simplicity's sake) is discovered drinking with Mr Kurgela, at whose house Eva has been awaiting them for the past three days. It is he rather than the judge whom Puntila harangues and tells to 'Wake up, weakling' (p. 5), continuing 'I realise you're only drinking with me because I've got a mortgage on your estate.' The judge, by his own account, is more abstemious because of his job. The passage about walking on the aquavit is not in the first script or the W–B version; the latter, incidentally, has them drinking cognac.

After Puntila has described his attacks, ending 'Look at the lack of consideration I've shown you' (p. 8), Kalle asks what sort of state he is in when signing his highly profitable timber contracts. A state of senseless sobriety, answers Puntila:

> When I'm a human being and having a drink then I only discuss art. If a timber merchant came along asking 'Can't you bring the price down?' I'd say 'No, you rascal, today I'm only discussing art. Today I like nice people, whoever they are.'

Matti's long speech about seeing ghosts, which ensues, underwent some reworking, while after 'Mr Pappmann yelled and screamed at me' (p. 8) it originally went on:

> – saying he'd tell the police about me, and that I should go to the
> Pferdeberg and have a good look at the piles of Reds who were
> shot there because it was what they asked for.
> PUNTILA: I've got nothing against socialists [originally: Marxists]
> so long as they drive my tractor . . .

and so on as on p. 9.

In the fair copy the speech ends with a much longer excursion about
the Reds before going on to Puntila's 'So the only reason you lost your
job' (p. 9) as at present. In the W–B version much of the speech is like
a paraphrase of the present text, relating not to Mr Pappmann's estate
but to 'the agronomist's at Kortesoja' where the trouble was not so
much the food as the clock-watching and general stinginess. Probably
the whole speech derived from one of Hella Wuolijoki's stories.

In Puntila's speech the reference to Mrs Klinckmann (p. 9) is not
in the three early versions, which have him saying 'and I've got woods'
rather than 'I shan't give up my forest.' The first script made him
allude to the day when he 'married a papermill and a sawmill' in
explanation of his evident prosperity. All three early versions then cut
straight from Matti's 'no gulf' (p. 10) to Puntila's instruction 'there,
take my wallet' (p. 11), the intervening dialogue about Mrs
Klinckmann and the sale of the forest only being introduced in the
1950 text. At the end of the scene the W–B version has the two men
wake the comatose Kurgela, who says he won't drive home as he is
frightened of Hanna. Puntila responds 'Down with all Hannas' and
gets Kalle to echo this.

Scene 2

The title of this scene on the first script, followed by W–B, was
'Puntila and his daughter Eva', on the fair copy 'Puntila is ill-treated',
and in the 1950 text 'Eva' as now. Originally Eva was discovered
reading, not munching chocolates, and the Attaché entered left, not
from an upper level.

The opening allusions to Mrs Klinckmann were added to the first
script, which originally started with the Attaché's 'I have telephoned
again.' His next speech, after 'it's got to be father' (p. 12) was

ATTACHÉ: Regrettable, yes.

EVA: Aunt Hanna is in such a bad mood. Imagine Father leading Uncle Kurgela astray.

ATTACHÉ: Aunt Hanna will forgive him. What disturbs me is the scandal.

– suggesting that, despite her changed role, Hanna is still being seen as part of the Attaché's family. Then on as on p. 12, up to Puntila's entrance. In all except the final text the latter 'bursts through the door in his Studebaker [or Buick in the W–B version] with a great crash and drives into the hall'; he also gets into the car again when preparing to leave. The allusions to Mrs Klinckmann on pp. 14–15 were to Aunt Hanna in the W–B version, where after 'And not getting a woman!' (p. 15) Puntila tells Eva 'I'm going, and Kalle's going to be your fiancé!'

After Eva's 'I won't have you speaking about your master like that' (p. 15) both the first script and W–B have Kalle saying that he is on the contrary sticking up for Puntila against Eva. He then asks Eva if she wants to get away, and is told he is being inquisitive. This leads him to discuss inquisitiveness, saying 'it was pure inquisitiveness that led to the invention of electricity. The Russians were inquisitive too.' Eva continues 'And don't take what he said' etc., as now, up to the present end of the scene. The W–B version prolongs this by making Eva reply to Kalle's last remark, 'You forget you're a servant.'

KALLE: After midnight I'm not a servant, I'm a man. (*Eva runs off*) Don't be afraid.

ATTACHÉ (*entering*): Who are you, fellow?

KALLE: Mr Iso-Heikkilä's chauffeur, sir.

The Attaché takes a dislike to him and threatens to check up on his past record. Kalle replies that he has been talking to the ghosts of departed ladies of Kurgela: 'I'm a sort of substitute bridegroom. Good night.'

Scene 3

The fair copy specifies at the outset that 'a tune like "Valencia" is being played'. In all three early versions Puntila starts by rousing a 'fat woman at the window', then the chemist's assistant, and has a bawling match with both before being sent on to the vet and picking up (virtually) the present text from p. 18. Emma appears after he has been given his prescription; in the first script and W–B she has no song; in the fair copy it is tacked on at the end of the play. Otherwise the rest of the scene follows very much as now, though each woman's description of her life is an evident addition to the original script. These accounts could well originate in stories told by Hella Wuolijoki, though in the W–B version there are some differences: thus the milkmaid does get meat, while the telephonist has 'enough money for pork dripping, potatoes, and salt herring' and gets a box of chocolates from the doctor.

Scene 4

In the three early scripts this follows the bath-hut scene, the present scene 5. The first script and fair copy limit Puntila's opening speech to 'I'm through with you', followed by the last sentence ('You took advantage' etc., p. 36). In the W–B version the setting is a 'hiring fair at Hollolan Lahei, a small park with a café, right. Left, a coffee stall with table and benches. Men are standing in scattered groups, the farmers are selecting labourers. Two stable girls giggling, left. Enter a fat man, left.' When the latter comments that there is not much doing, a labourer explains that people prefer to take forestry jobs, since the wages are going up there. Then Puntila enters, and the sense of what follows is much the same as in Brecht's script. In both, however, the proposed conditions of work are less bad than in the final version: the redhaired man is promised his meals and a potato patch, while the (first) worker is told that he will get wood delivered. In all three of these scripts Puntila's first speech after sitting down to coffee (p. 27) tells Kalle/Matti that he must control himself with respect to Eva, and it is this that Matti answers by 'Just let it be', after which the scene continues as now for about half a page. However, Surkkala (p. 28.) is Salminen in the W–B version, and the reason why the parson wanted him thrown out was not because he was a Red but 'because he has a wife he's not married to, and appears suspect to the National Militia in various other ways.' All three versions of the scene end with Puntila's 'make me respect you' (p. 30).

Scene 5

In all three early scripts this precedes the hiring fair scene. All are headed 'Puntila [or Iso-Heikkilä] betroths his daughter to an Attaché', as in the plan. All omit the arrival of the labourers from the hiring fair and place Puntila's sobering-up process in the bath at the beginning of scene 6. They set the present scene not on Puntila's estate but at Kurgela

> with a bath-hut that can be seen into. Kalle sits whistling beneath some sunflowers as he cleans a carburettor. Beside him the housekeeper [or in W–B the maid Miina] with a basket. It is morning.

HOUSEKEEPER: Kindly have look at the door. Last night when you drove the Studebaker into the hall you ripped off the hinges.

KALLE: Can be managed; but don't blame that door business on me; it's him that was drunk.

HOUSEKEEPER: But if he sees it today he'll be furious. He always inspects the whole estate and checks every corner of our barns, because he holds our mortgage.

KALLE: Yes, he's fussy; he doesn't like things to be in a mess.

HOUSEKEEPER (leaving): The mistress is staying in bed with a headache because she'd just as soon not run into him. We're all nervous so long as he's here; he shouts so.

PUNTILA'S VOICE: Tina! Tina! [or in W–B, 'Miina!']

KALLE (to the housekeeper as she tries to go): I'd stay where you are; he's amazingly quick on his feet and if you try to get away he'll spot you.

PUNTILA (entering) [accompanied by Kurgela in W–B]: There you are; I've been looking all over the house for you. I'm tired of having showdowns with you people, you're ruining yourselves in any case; but when I see things like the way you preserve pork it sends me up the wall. Come Christmas you chuck it away, and the same goes for your forest and all the rest. You're a lazy crew, and you figure I'll go on paying till kingdom come. Look at the gardener going around with patched trousers; well, I wouldn't complain if it was his knees that were patched and not his bottom. If it's a gardener the knees of his trousers ought to be patched.

And the egg ledger has too many inkblots over the figures. Why? Because you can't imagine why there are so few eggs. Of course it has never dawned on you that the dairymaid might be swiping the eggs; you need me to tell you. And don't just hang around here all day!

(*The housekeeper leaves in a hurry*)

PUNTILA (*in the doorway*): Got you, boyo.

– and so into the episode with the wallet (p. 35). Then after Matti's third 'Yes, Mr Puntila' (p. 36) Puntila leaves and Eva appears (out of the bath-hut in the first script and carrying a towel) asking 'But why don't you stick up for yourself?' etc., thus cutting out the exchange between Puntila and the two workers. The Eva–Matti dialogue and the ensuing bath-hut charade then follow very much as in our text, but with the Kurgela housekeeper of course instead of Laina. In the W–B version Kalle has gathered from Eva's father that the attaché is to be got rid of, and so the six lines from Eva's 'that he must be the one to back out' to 'I'm crude' (p. 37) are missing, as is Matti's ensuing speech 'Well, suppose' with its allusion to Tarzan. Otherwise there are only very slight differences between all three versions and the final text.

Scene 6

The three early scripts have the title 'What Kalle [Matti] is and is not prepared to do.' As later, the scene is set in the Puntila kitchen, but begins with the sobering-up episode that was later shifted to scene 5 (pp. 34–35). Thus the first script:

> *Farm Kitchen at Puntila Hall. Kalle is trying to sober Puntila up by pouring cold water over his head. The weedy man is sitting in a corner. It is late evening.*

There is music. The scene starts with Matti's 'You'll have to bear with a few buckets' (p. 32); then after 'that fat man at the hiring fair' and before Fina's entry Puntila goes on:

> . . . by the car, he was just going to collect the piglet and missed it. That's enough buckets, I never have more than eleven. (*Shouts*)

Fina! Coffee!

(*Enter Fina*)

PUNTILA: Here's that golden creature with my coffee.

FINA: Miss Hanna says wouldn't you rather take your coffee in the drawing-room; Kalle can have his here.

PUNTILA: I'm staying here. If Kalle isn't good enough for her I'm having my coffee in the kitchen. Where is it?

FINA *goes and produces coffee from the stove*: Here you are, Mr Puntila.

PUNTILA: Is it good and strong? . . .

Then, after Kalle/Matti's 'No liqueur,' Puntila says to hell with his guests, Fina must hear the story of the fat man, which he then recounts, starting from 'One of those nasty fat individuals' (though 'a proper capitalist' is not in the early scripts). The rest of the episode is virtually as in our text except that after Puntila's second coffee (p. 34) Matti's speech about love of animals, with its reference to Mrs Klinckmann, is replaced by the exchange between him and the weedy man which is now on pp. 31–32 ff. immediately after Puntila has gone into the bath-hut. Thereafter it is Kalle who asks Puntila if the coffee was strong enough, and the remainder down to 'despise me when he's pissed' (p. 35) is as in our text.

The link between the sobering-up episode and the present beginning of the scene (p. 44) was simply a ring on the bell, leading Fina to say 'I forgot to say Miss Eva wants a word with you.' Then Hanna (or Alina) comes in – after the eighteen-line dialogue between Matti and Fina, ending with her sitting on his lap, which is all cut in W–B – and tells Fina to tidy the library and take the weedy man to the room where he is to spend the night prior to leaving; he must also return his 100 marks earnest money (most such sums being divided by ten in the course of revision). On his complaining that he has lost two days' work Hanna blames Kalle. Then the judge and lawyer (replaced by Agronomist Kurgela in W–B) come in, after which the rest of the scene continues much as in our text. However, the first two stage directions (pp. 46–47) describing Eva's would-be seductive walk were added later, while the third (on her re-entering on p. 47) originally read 'wearing sandals and pretty shorts.'

Scene 7

With the exception of Emma's last speech with its snatch of song (p. 59) and her action of sitting on the ground, this scene has remained essentially as it was when Brecht first wrote it, as envisaged in the preliminary plans. Among the small modifications incorporated in the 1950 version (and thereafter in our text) are the conception of the two-level set, the Sunday atmosphere with its bells, Puntila's phrase about the wedding costing him a forest (p. 52), the women's straw garlands and Matti's haranguing of the broom. In all three early versions Puntila's remark about forming a trade union (p. 58) is answered by Matti: 'Excuse me, Mr Puntila, it's not a trade union because there are no dues. So nobody's interests are represented. It was just for a bit of a laugh and maybe for a cup of coffee.' Finally in lieu of Emma's last speech the telephonist tells Puntila:

> But it's only a joke. You invited us yourself . . .
> EMMA: You have no right to say we wanted to blackmail you.
> PUNTILA: Get off my land!

End of scene.

Scene 8

This had no title before the 1950 version. In the first script it is unnumbered but inserted separately from scene 7, which suggests that it was added later; it is followed by a photograph of a peasant woman. In the fair copy it is numbered 7a, and in the W–B version 'Scene 7, conclusion, to be played on the forestage.' Emma's first tale (starting 'the last police sergeant's wife') is not in W–B; the telephonist's tale ('They know what they're up to') is delivered by the dairymaid; and the latter's ('Me too' p. 61) is spoken by the peasant woman in the first script and by Emma in W–B. This is then followed by a comment from the telephonist 'What fools we women are,' which in W–B ends the scene. The first script adds Emma's long story (pp. 61–62) but gives it to the telephonist.

Scene 9 [8 in the early scripts]

Again the title and general sense of the scene have remained unchanged ever since Brecht's first plans, though a long section was cut out of its middle (which somewhat alters the picture of Eva) while the ending with Red Surkkala's song was tacked on to the fair copy. Originally the opening conversation was among parson, judge, doctor and lawyer (or agronomist in W–B); there was a slight redistribution and cutting of lines once the doctor had been eliminated. At first too the Attaché appeared accompanied not only by the parson's wife but also by Hanna/Alina, who delivered what are now the parson's wife's lines, sighed, and left.

The major change occurred after the parson's wife's reproachful cry of 'Eva!' (p. 68), before Puntila reappears. Here there enter, not Puntila at first but

> *the cook and Fina the maid with a great basket full of bottles. They clear the dining table and place them on it.*

EVA: What are you doing, Fina?

FINA: Master told us to reset the table.

PARSON'S WIFE: Are you saying that he came to the kitchen?

THE COOK: Yes, he was in a hurry, looking for the chauffeur.

EVA: Has the Attaché driven away?

FINA: I think so.

EVA: Why can't people say things for certain? I hate this awful uncertainty all round me.

FINA *laughing*: My guess is that you're not sorry, Miss Eva.

(*Enter Puntila and Kalle, followed by the doctor*)

PUNTILA: Hear that, Eva? There was I, sitting over my punch, thinking about nothing in particular, when suddenly I caught myself looking at the fellow and wondering how the devil anyone could have a face like that. I blinked and wondered if my eyesight had gone wrong, so I had another glass and looked again, and then of course I knew what I had to do. What are all you people on your feet for?

PARSON: Mr Puntila, I thought that since the party's over we ought to take our leave. You must be tired, Anna.

PUNTILA: Rubbish. You're not going to resent one of old Puntila's jokes, not like that pettifogging lawyer Kallios who keeps picking holes in everything I do and just at the very instant when I've realised my mistake and want to put it right; yes, the Attaché was a flop but I did a good job once I'd caught on, you'll bear me out there. Puntila may go off the rails, but not for long before he sees it and becomes quite human again. You found the wine? Take a glass and let's all sit down; I'll just tell the others there's been a mistake and the engagement party's going on. If that Attaché – scavenger, that's what he is, and I'm amazed you didn't realise it right away, Eva, – as I was saying, if he imagines he can screw up my engagement after weeks of preparation then he can think again. The fact is I decided a long time ago to marry my daughter to a good man, Matti Altonen, a fine chauffeur and a good friend of mine. Fina, hurry up and tell whoever's dancing in the park that they're to come here as soon as the dance is over; there've been some interesting changes. I'll go and get the minister. (*Goes out*)

KALLE: Your father's going too far, even allowing for him being drunk.

EVA: [illegible]

KALLE: I'm amazed you let him treat you like that in public.

EVA: I like being an obedient daughter.

KALLE: He's going to be disappointed, though. Maybe he can give your hand to anyone he chooses, but he can't give mine, and that includes giving it to you.

Eva answers 'Don't look at me' etc., as on p. 69, down to Matti's 'it wasn't to get married', after which she continues:

I don't believe you. That wasn't how you held me at Kurgela. You're like Hulda down in the village, who had five illegitimate children with a fellow and then when they asked why she didn't marry him she said 'I don't like him.'

KALLE: Stop laughing, and stop telling dirty stories. You're drunk. I can't afford to marry you.

EVA: With a sawmill you could.

KALLE: I already told you I'm not playing Victor to you. If he wants to scatter sawmills around he can give them to you, not to me. He's human enough when he's stewed but when he's sober he's sharp. He'll spend a million on an attaché for you but not on a chauffeur.

(*Parson, judge, parson's wife and doctor have been standing as a group in the background and putting their heads together. Now the parson goes up to Eva*)

PARSON: Eva, my dear, I must speak to you like when I was preparing you for confirmation. [An illegible line is added.] Mr Altonen is welcome to stay, in view of his unfortunate involvement. Eva my dear, it is your hard duty to tell your father in no uncertain terms that he cannot dispose of you like a heifer and that God has given you a will of your own.

EVA: That would conflict with my obedience to parental authority, your Reverence.

PARSON: It is a higher form of obedience, an obedience that goes against accepted morality.

KALLE: That's just what I say.

PARSON: I am glad you have so much good sense. It makes the situation considerably easier for you, my child.

EVA: What's so hard about it? I shall say to my father in bell-like tones: I propose to do as you command. I am going to marry Kalle. Even if it means risking his saying in front of everybody that he doesn't want me.

KALLE: If you ask me, the problem's a lot simpler than that, your Reverence. I think he'll have forgotten all about it by the time he comes back here. I'll be the sacrifice and go into the kitchen with him, we'll have a bottle or two and I'll tell him how I've been sacked from job after job, that's something he likes hearing about.

EVA: If you do that I'll go into the kitchen too.

PARSON: I am sadly disappointed in you, Eva. (*He goes back to the others*) It's unbelievable. She's determined to marry the man.

DOCTOR: In that case it's time I went; I'd rather not be present; I know Puntila. (*Goes out*)

PARSON: All I can say is that I'd leave too if I didn't feel it my duty to drain this cup to the dregs.

PARSON'S WIFE: Besides, Mr Puntila would be displeased. (*The dance music next door suddenly stops. A confused sound of voices which likewise stops after a moment. The ensuing silence allows one to hear the accordion playing for the dancers in the park*)

KALLE: You're taking advantage of the situation.

EVA: I want my husband to be a man.

KALLE: What you want is a lively evening, never mind what anyone else may think. You're your father's daughter all right.

(*Enter Puntila by himself, angry*)

PUNTILA (*taking a bottle from the table and drinking from it*): I have just had a profound insight . . .

and so on as on p. 68. Then there is a cut straight from his 'Fina, you come and sit by me' (p. 69) straight to *All sit down reluctantly* (thirteen lines below).

Thereafter there are only small differences in the scene at the table with Matti testing Eva. One is that Puntila's query 'Matti, can you fuck decently' (p. 70) down to Matti's 'Can we change the subject?' is not in the first script or the W–B version but was an addition to the fair copy. Then when Matti slaps Eva's behind both the first version and the fair copy have her evading the slap; she simply says 'How dare you,' etc. In the first version the scene ends with the exit of the cook and the parson's wife (p. 79). In the fair copy, however, Matti's immediately preceding speech continues after 'unforgiving':

> It's only that the kitchen staff will be here in a minute; the music has stopped. You made Fina call them to hear about some new development. What are you going to say when they get here, led by Miss Hanna with her sharp tongue?
>
> PUNTILA: I'll tell them that I've disowned my daughter for being a crime against Nature.
>
> MATTI: You might do better to tell them that tomorrow.

Then he turns 'to Laina and the parson's wife' as on p. 78 down to their exit, after which one hears singing from the dance off:

> The wolf asked the rooster a question:
> 'Shouldn't we get to know each other better
> Know and understand each other better?'
> The rooster thought that a good suggestion
> Must have responded to the question
> I'd say, seeing the field's full of feathers.
> Oh, Oh.
>
> The match asked the can a question:
> 'Shouldn't we get to know each other better
> Know and respect each other better?'

The can thought that a good suggestion
Must have responded to the question
I'd say, seeing the sky's turning crimson.

The boss asked the maid a question:
Shouldn't we get to know each other better
Know and respect each other better?
The maid thought that a good suggestion
Must have responded to the question
I'd say, seeing her stays are bulging.
Oh, oh.

PUNTILA: That's meant for me. Songs like that cut me to the quick.

The last stage direction first appears in the 1950 text. Red Surkkala's song was added at the end of the fair copy, developing the theme of the first stanza of the above, then in the 1950 version supplanted it.

Scene 10

This is not in the W–B version but is included in the first script with no scene number or title. In the fair copy it is numbered 8a.

Scene 11 [9 in the early scripts]

In the first script the title is 'Puntila and Kalle climb Mount Hatelma', in the fair copy 'Puntila sits in judgement and climbs Mount Hatelma', in the W–B version 'Iso-Heikkilä condemns Kalle.' The setting in the first script is the

Library at Puntila Hall. Hanna, the old housekeeper, is writing out accounts, when Puntila sticks his head in, with a towel round it. He is about to draw back when he sees that Hanna has observed him, and walks across the room to the door. On her addressing him he is painfully affected and stops.

HANNA: Mr Puntila, I have to talk to you. Now don't pretend you've got something important to do, and don't look so pained. For the past week I've said nothing because what with the engagement and the house guests I've had my hands so full I didn't know where I was. But now the time has come. Do you realise what you've done?

PUNTILA: Hanna, I have a dreadful headache. I think if I had another cup of coffee and a bit of a nap it might help; what do you think?

HANNA: I think you've needed something quite different and been needing it a long time. Do you realise that his honour the judge has left?

PUNTILA: What, Fredrik? That seems childish.

HANNA: Do you expect him to stay in a place the foreign minister's been thrown out of? Not to mention the Attaché, who moves in the very best circles and will be telling everybody about you? You'll be left sitting at Puntila Hall like a lone rhinoceros. Society will shun you.

PUNTILA: I can't understand that minister. He sees I'm a bit boozed, and then goes and takes everything I say literally.

HANNA: You've always made a nuisance of yourself, but ever since that chauffeur came to the estate it's been too much. Twenty years I've been at the manor, but now you're going to have to make up your mind: it's the chauffeur or me.

PUNTILA: What are you talking about? You can't go. Who'd run the business? I've got such a headache, I think I'm getting pneumonia. Imagine attacking a man in such an inhuman way.

HANNA: I'll expect your answer. (*Turns towards the door*)

PUNTILA: You people grudge me even the smallest pleasure. Get me some milk, my head's bursting.

HANNA: There won't be any milk for you. The cook's passed out too, she was drunk. Here come the parson and the doctor.

PUNTILA: I don't want to see them, my health isn't up to it. (*Hanna opens the door to the two gentlemen*)

PARSON: Good morning, Mr Puntila, I trust that you had a restful night. (*Puntila mumbles something*) I ran into the doctor on the road; we thought we'd drop in and see how you were.

PUNTILA (*dubiously*): I see.

DOCTOR: Rough night, what? I'd drink some milk if I were you.

PARSON: My wife asked to be remembered to you. She and Miss Laina had a most interesting talk.

(*Pause*)

PARSON (*gingerly*): I'm very much surprised to hear Miss Hanna is thinking of leaving.

PUNTILA: Where did you hear that?

PARSON: Where? Oh, I really couldn't say. You know how these rumours get around.

PUNTILA: By telephone, I suppose. I'd like to know who phoned you.

PARSON: I assure you, Mr Puntila, there was no question of anybody phoning. What made me call was simply being upset that someone so universally respected as Miss Hanna should be forced to take such a step.

DOCTOR: I told you it was a misunderstanding.

PUNTILA: I'd just like to know who has been telephoning people from here behind my back. I know these coincidences.

DOCTOR: Don't be difficult, Puntila. Nothing's being done behind your back. We're not having this conversation behind your back, are we?

PUNTILA: If I find you've been intriguing against me, Finstrand, I'll put you on *your* back soon enough.

PARSON: Mr Puntila, this is getting us nowhere. I must ask you to consider our words as words of friendship because we've heard you were losing the valuable services of Miss Hanna, and it's very hard to imagine what the estate would do without her.

DOCTOR: If you want to throw us out like yesterday, go right ahead. You can put up a barbed-wire fence around the estate and drink yourself to death behind it.

PUNTILA (*with hostility*): So somebody did phone.

DOCTOR: Oh God, yes. Do you think everyone in Lammi just takes it for granted when you insult a cabinet minister under your own roof and drive your daughter's fiancé off the estate by stoning him?

PUNTILA: What's that about stoning? I'd like to know who's spreading that stoning story.

PARSON: Mr Puntila, let's not waste time on details. I fear I have come to the conclusion that much of what happened yesterday is not at all clear in your memory. For instance, I doubt whether you are aware of the exact wording of the insults which you hurled after our foreign minister, Mr Puntila.

DOCTOR: It may interest you to know that you called him a shit.

PUNTILA: That's an exaggeration.

PARSON: Alas, no. Perhaps that will make you realise that when you are in that deplorable condition you don't always act as you might think wise in retrospect. You risk incurring considerable damage.

PUNTILA: Any damage I incur is paid for by me, not you.

DOCTOR: True. But there is some damage which you can't pay for.

PARSON: Which money cannot repair.

DOCTOR: Though it's the first time I've seen you take things so lightly when somebody like Miss Hanna gives notice in the middle of the harvest.

PARSON: We should overlook such material considerations, doctor. I've known Mr Puntila to be just as understanding where purely moral considerations were concerned. It might not be unrewarding to take the matter of Surkkala as an example of the dangers of over-indulgence in alcohol, and discuss it with Mr Puntila in a friendly, dignified spirit.

PUNTILA: What about Surkkala?

All this long introduction, which was replaced by the present text in the 1950 version, takes us only to p. 82, after which the scene continues as now as far as Puntila's shaking of the parson's hand on p. 83, apart of course from the giving of Laina's lines to Hanna.

Thereafter the parson, before leaving, begs Hanna not to abandon her employer but to go on acting as his guardian angel; to which she replies: 'That depends on Mr Puntila.' The doctor advises him to drink less, and the two men go out. Puntila's ensuing speech about giving up drinking ('Laina, from now on' etc.) is addressed to Hanna, not Laina, and is somewhat shorter than now. In the W–B version it follows straight after Hanna's statement that the cook was drunk (p. 148 above), the whole episode with the parson and the doctor/lawyer being thus omitted. To return to the first script, Hanna then replies:

Liquor and low company are to blame. I'll send for that criminal chauffeur, you can deal with him for a start. (*Calls through the doorway*) Kalle! Come into the library at once!

PUNTILA: That Surkkala business is a lesson to me; imagine my not evicting him. That's what happens once you let the demon rum get a toe-hold.

Surkkala's appearance with his family is omitted, Kalle/Matti entering at this point with his 'Good morning, Mr Puntila,' etc. as on p. 84. He then has to defend himself not to Puntila (and against the accusations of the latter's friends) but to Hanna, to whom he says that he was merely carrying out instructions and (as in the final text) could not confine himself to the sensible ones (p. 84).

HANNA: There's no need to top it all by being impertinent. They told me how you chased after your master's daughter at Kurgela and pestered her in the bath-hut.

KALLE: Only for the sake of appearances.

HANNA: You do everything for the sake of appearances. You put on a show of zeal and manage to get yourself ordered to force your lustful attentions on your employer's daughter and smoke Puntila's cigars. Who invited those Kurgela creatures over to Puntila Hall?

KALLE: Mr Puntila, down in the village at half-past four a.m.

HANNA: Yes, but who worked them up and got them to come into the house where the foreign minister was being entertained? You.

PUNTILA: I caught him trying to make them ask me for money for breach of promise.

HANNA: And then the hiring fair?

PUNTILA: He frightened off the redhaired man I was after and landed me with that weedy fellow I had to send packing because he scared the cows.

KALLE: Yes, Mr Puntila.

HANNA: As for the engagement party last night . . . You ought to have the whole estate on your conscience. There's Miss Eva sitting upstairs with a headache and a broken heart for the rest of her life, when she could have been happily married in three or four months' time.

KALLE: All I can say, Miss Hanna, is that if I hadn't restrained myself something much worse would have happened.

HANNA: You and she were sitting in the kitchen on Saturday night, do you deny that?

KALLE: We had a perfectly harmless conversation which I am not going to describe to you in detail, Miss Hanna, you being a spinster, and I don't mean that as an insult but as my personal conclusion based on certain pieces of evidence that are not relevant to the present discussion.

HANNA: So you're dropping your hypocritical mask, you Bolshevik. It all comes of your boozing with creatures like this, Mr Puntila, and not keeping your distance. I'm leaving.

Puntila then tells Matti/Kalle, in much the same words as now used to Laina on p. 83, to bring out all the bottles containing liquor so that they may be smashed. He follows with a shorter version of his speech on p. 85 down to 'Too few people are aware of that', after which Matti reappears with the bottles. The dialogue is close to that of our text, but with Hanna/Alina fulfilling Laina's role of trying to stop Puntila drinking, until he turns on her (p. 86) after his 'I never want to see it again, you heard.' Then instead of going on as in our text he says:

> And don't contradict me, woman; you're my evil genius. That gaunt face of yours makes me sick. I can't even get a drink of milk when I'm sick, and in my own house too. Because there you are, telephoning everyone behind my back and bringing in the parson to treat me like a schoolboy; I won't have it. Your pettiness has been poisoning my life for the last thirty years. I can't bear pettiness, you rusty old adding machine.

Then come four lines as in our text from 'You lot want me to rot away here' to 'tot up the cattle feed', continuing:

> I look across the table, and what do I see but you, you sleazy piece of black crape. I'm giving you notice, do you hear?
>
> HANNA: That beats everything. The two of you getting drunk before my very eyes!
>
> PUNTILA: Get out.
>
> HANNA: Are you trying to give *me* notice? Here's the man you promised you'd give notice to. You promised the parson himself. You were going to report him to the authorities. (*Puntila laughs, picks her up and carries her out, cursing him at the top of her voice*) Wastrel! Drunkard! Tramp!
>
> PUNTILA (*returning*): That got rid of her.

Matti/Kalle's speech 'I hope the punch is all right,' etc. follows as on

p. 86, together with Puntila's next speech as far as 'a calamity all the same.' Then instead of the reference to Surkkala and the half-page of dialogue with him and his family Puntila runs straight on:

> I always said it takes a certain inner strength to keep on the right path.
>
> KALLE: You always get more out of it if you wander off, Mr Puntila. Practically everything that's at all pleasant lies off the right path, you'd almost think the right path had been thought up on purpose to discourage people.
>
> PUNTILA: I say the pleasant path is the right one. And in my opinion you're a good guide. Just looking at you makes me thirsty.
>
> KALLE: I'd like to say something about yesterday's engagement party, Mr Puntila. There were one or two misunderstandings due to the impossibility of suppressing human nature, but if I may say so inhuman nature can't be suppressed either. You rather underrated the gulf between me and Miss Eva until I tickled her backside; I suppose it was because offhand you didn't see why I shouldn't go catching crayfish with Miss Eva just as well as the next man, which is an offhand way of looking at the sexes and one that doesn't get under the surface – as if only the intimate things mattered and not upbringing. As far as I know, though, nothing that happened at the party was so disastrous that you can't put it right, though all that came of it really was that the parson's wife now knows how to preserve mushrooms.
>
> PUNTILA: I can't take it tragically. Looking at it from the broad point of view, not from a petty one; devil take the woman, she's got a petty outlook, she's nothing. Eva will inherit the estate even if she makes a bad marriage.
>
> KALLE: Even if. Because so long as she's got the estate, and the cows yield milk and there's someone to drive the milk churns to the co-operative and they keep an eye on the grain and so on, nothing else counts. Whether it's a good or bad marriage isn't going to prevent her from selling her trees. You can chop down a forest even with a broken heart.

Then Puntila asks what his pay is, as on p. 89 (though the amount varies from script to script) and goes on, as in our text, to propose

climbing Mount Hatelma. After his 'We could do it in spirit' (p. 88)
Matti/Kalle interposes in the first script (not in W–B):

> In spirit is always much the simplest way. I once got sore at an
> Englishman for parking his car so stupidly that I had to shove it
> out of the way with my drunken boss sitting in the Ford cursing
> me. In spirit I declared war on England, I defeated them in spirit,
> brought them to their knees, and laid down stiff peace terms; it
> was all very simple, I remember.

Then Puntila finishes with 'Given a chair or two we could' etc. (p. 88)
and the dialogue continues virtually as we have it for some two pages,
omitting only the stage direction on p. 88 with its mention of the
billiard table. After Puntila's 'Are you a Tavastlander?' (p. 89),
however, Kalle gave details, e.g., from the first script:

> Originally, yes. I was born the other side of those forests in a
> cabin by the lake, and I grew up on bare stony ground.
> PUNTILA: Hold on, let's take it all in proper order. First and
> foremost, where else is there a sky . . .

– and so on as in our text to the end of the scene. In the W–B version
there are some cuts, and Kalle adds after his present concluding line
'Long live Tavastland and its Iso-Heikkilä!' after which the two men
sing the lines about the Roina once again. (These come from the
nineteenth-century poet Topelius, and the Roina is a lake in central
Finland.)

Scene 12 [10 in the first script]

Laina's second speech and both Matti's first two were additions on the
fair copy. In the first script, after Laina's 'until Mr Puntila's up' (p.
92) Kalle continues:

> I'm glad I was able to straighten out that business with the
> housekeeper. It got me a settlement of two months' pay, and she
> was so glad to be rid of me she gave me a decent reference.
> COOK: I don't get it. When you're in so good with the master.
> KALLE: That's just the problem. I couldn't have *him* writing a
> reference for me; I'd never get another job so long as I lived.

Then as in our text from Laina's 'He won't be able to manage without you' to her exit, after which Kalle flings a stone at one of the balcony windows and Eva appears in night attire.

> EVA: What's up? Why have you got your suitcase?
> KALLE: I'm leaving.
> EVA (*after a pause*): Why do you want to leave?
> KALLE: I can't stay for ever.
> EVA: I'm sorry you're going, Kalle.
> KALLE: I'll send you a crayfish for your birthday.
> EVA: I'd sooner you came back yourself.
> KALLE: Right. In a year from now.
> EVA: I'll wait that long.
> KALLE: By then I'll have my sawmill.
> EVA: Fine. I'll have learned how to darn socks by then.
> KALLE: Then it will work. Bye.
> EVA: Bye. (*Goes back into her room*)

The epilogue follows with some very slight variations.

The W–B version tacks this scene on to the preceding one by having Eva enter and call Puntila down from his mountain, after which he goes off with Fina and Laina, leaving her and Kalle alone. She asks 'Why have you got your suitcase?' as above, but the dialogue differs from that in the first script by having her press him to make it less than a year and suggesting that her father might give her a sawmill. Kalle says he will send her books, and she agrees to read them; then she comes close to him, forcing him to say 'Go away and lead me not into temptation.' He pushes her off, and the epilogue follows.